Da Via is a former successful businessman, who after an unconventional Harvard education, developed his interest in China. He is also the author of *Moneydie*.

To John, Marion, Al and Khalil

Da Via

ART FOR WAR

AUSTIN MACAULEY PUBLISHERS™

LONDON • CAMBRIDGE • NEW YORK • SHARJAH

A CIP catalogue record for this title is available from the British Library.

ISBN 9781528911641 (Paperback)
ISBN 9781528911658 (Hardback)
ISBN 9781528959858 (ePub e-book)

www.austinmacauley.com

First Published (2020)
Austin Macauley Publishers Ltd
25 Canada Square
Canary Wharf
London
E14 5LQ

In writing *Art for War,* there were a number of people who helped me with good advice. The Chinese visual artist, Ruoxuan Zhao, and the Chinese poet, Cigeng. David Ramsden. Harvard University for a superb unorthodox education in classics and China in general. And, most of all, my family and friends for all of their love and support.

Introduction

Before he died, Umberto Eco said that the universe's first and greatest conspiracy is the books of the establishment of the western literary tradition.

What follows is an ancient secret text first written long, long ago and updated periodically until the time of the Tang Dynasty. The Tang was a period of great intellectual and cultural flourishing in the orient, whilst the west remained shackled to the Dark Ages.

The ancient Chinese considered the human body to consist of two hundred and fourteen bones, and to each bone, a radical character was prescribed. For the purposes of our narrative, the pelvic and lumbar bones are of the greatest significance.

We brought the Dark Ages
Upon the husbands
Those Barbarian Heroes
The Summer Dogs of War
In song and tuned,
For we are the dolphins
The kings who stole time
By Art for War,
And Also.

Chapter One

The Use of Eyes
and Contemplation

§1.1

A piece of meat in the sun: former days, bygone.

From ancient times, a cover was set a top the Hostages of the Sun.

That the Lu would not worry over the sun and moon of verses nor vocabulary nor syntaxes in the poetry of the past. And so the Lu did not think of former days, nor the forms that shaped their minds from before "bi" was gone; nor why we did this to her of old.

The Lu, as if thick woods grew, strung along by unclear words, of thorny brushes, giving nothing but distress.

And so, heroes originated, spun, unquestioned by the dazed, as if validated representatives of the dead. The Lu took what they were offered and made a sacrifice of the meat, in return causing their own extinction to sound and smell and patterns.

Anciently, the oriental kings served their fathers by intelligence.

Defining love of wisdom in ordered thoughts and words.

Floating these powerful creations upwards.

As if gliding birds, soaring the heads of men.

For whom those notions of words served as heaven. Yet those words paired and corresponded to radical characters, each to an ancestral bone, used to express thoughts and by pairing, ideas. And then we used those characters as words for the many simplified, and thereby invented the art of disguising our thoughts and lies our strength and our weapon. In the struggle in a process of persuading the many that such things of great value have none, by confusion in the muddle of a babble.

Sewing eyes by silken threads from the rosy dawn of civilisation and making murky what should be clarity.

Inventing the school of the school.

Teaching the surgery of catching wide eyes programmed by the details of the case and the truth they wished allured by that famous serpent.

For there are people, who mind minds for the sake of currency concealed in honours and dependency.

Set and sealed by inherent nature.

Tailoring adjustments to controversy by clothing a science of long threaded division in winds twisted together as a weaving tool to tangle the disorderly in their silken network.

For the small table was obscured.

And so subtly the minds of the insolent Lu were invaded.

By a war considered fare for gold as payment for the passages, the journey, and the road.

Providing food and thereby a warfare for the few.

Inflaming the sickness that maintains a conceited calming, by purpose, in mystery.

For few know of this school.

Do not oppose the few.

Nor look at what is contrary to propriety.

Nor write of that, nor listen.

Yet as a scholar, accept now this support from a man of writing about what is not in accordance with such deceitful notions of propriety.

For herein is a gift.

For which I expect nothing in return. Other than for your use of making clear what is right.

And what is wrong in this world.

Learn the nature of this small table.

And read from those ancient heavenly forms that rose.

For the ancestors used Art for War.

And, by graduation, degree and initiation is the Art of the Establishment.

And so, the Way of the evil of the moment.

Forms are the spirits of music of the ancient songs that grandly roll thunder, and easy to follow, trust and sport confidence in.

You can depend on them; you can turn words around and thereby turn the body of the text.

Yet now they are corrupted, misty and clothed as a machine for dilution of juice by the small table of the few at the top.

For such is their purpose and then there are they who know not of this school.

And such is the nature of sound paper, the language of words, words of the moment, and the hearts of those people with the special look who own the hearts and minds of the Lu children.

Whom the Lu children love as if parents and who carry on the poetry and festival of Lu as if a rock show provided for the world they are killing.

Lost, the Lu people are lost, scattered and contrary to the in verses the Lu celebrate as hits.

For They are in addition and Also and the component of the fork in the way of agitation.

For They are the worn out public, and thereby the victims of the complex questions of express contrast.

And of the promise to thrive and prosper.

Unaware of the medicine.

And the radical bones of contention.

For that is the Thing.

And so you will read of the people, governance and the pie.

The components of the Babel school, the wood, the fat of the meat and thus the Imperial instructions for the original texts and poetry to be changed by a secret concordance whereby the conceit was invented and words became power.

As if sincerely, cordially and warm, yet to grease Li by the hand of the executive and the ceremony of deleted words, where there is a shortage loved.

For this was carried out by the music master Zhi and thereby the creation of Fortunately [that is by this cunning design our good fortune], by manmade formation as if even, and is the pill to cure the disease by the fist of pages, and the secret knowledge of the Word Cloud, without which understanding was impossible.

Thereby inflicting a disease of the mind and reason and therefore, a confusion in matters of the heart and soul, and such is the nature of the disease and the hidden hands at play in the slaughter of yesterday's generation.

All of which took place without the notion of a loss of neither justice nor recognition for the suffering it would cause.

Thereby nurturing was only possible with a guide that, a Sage in place was only possible for those who could afford. Therefore, the many people suffered from a good teacher. For an evil of man is that they like to be teachers of others and thereby hold the keys, giving the notions of the worthiest amongst them places of dignity and offices of trust.

Thereby summers are great by this common sacrifice to the god of war and therefore, leisure for the nobility.

And so, this is the story of the bone of contention, the Ilium and the hostages of the sun or Homers. The people we had the measure of and whose horses we harnessed to drive against the Lu. In for them an Iliad of chaos after we cut the sound by the division brigade, by head crosses, and the woman knot by a curse of evil words clever that we might gain a country from the sound of a horse.

Thereby Qi was the doctor's name, driving the lines to be cut in what we know as the ancient odd cut. Whereby the woman returned to our shelf from where to inflict flails and hold cabinet.

For such was the barbarian price for the false flag that we sold them. Granting our room for leisure by the Lu sacrifice to our god of war, for which we let them borrow, bested by the power of creation and cunning of the people of the East.

Thereby we could lean on those donkeys for whom brightness was cut, and they became scared to look for the loopholes and the threads. Fooled by the sound of the tigers we deceived in their heads by angry words.

And so, from there we cut logical reasoning, and the Lu became easy to surprise, and then we confused their calendar deceiving them further.

Then we stepped on legislation and invented fraud out of the code. Then from there we invented "At First Glance" and thereby cut the Lu further with the details of the language of "Thank You".

Then the Iliac bone did its work, the children became scared, yet tricky also, and so we laughed and sighed, and enjoyed our leisure and night schools.

Then we declared the Lu wooden and cut them seven.

Then we burnt the meat for the sunburnt, made the Son the guise of night, and thereby cut them further with a provision of an amnesty forgiveness should they ever work it out, or the nature of the horse by the cloud water of the North Hill.

We shot the Lu as vulgar tyrants of the cross by our bows in this crucial fiction and thereby bridled the leather in such clothing afraid of ghosts.

Yes, summer days for us at the Ministry of Military Science, from the people who know pages penned with the clause of both hands, and the old bone of contention. For without the keys to Imperial words, there is no ceremony, no system and no text, and thus no eyes.

For the bone of contention is the pelvis or ilium. As the Chinese phonetic word "gé" means both the science of change theory and sacrifice to the gods of war, and other things, as well as the Iliac. For by their sleepy behaviour the Lu sacrificed their knowledge of change theory from ancient times in a manner the Lu do not know.

For such is the sun and moon of these leaves, and the plumes and black-haired cone brushes of ancient times, and the calligraphy of the short-tailed birds of the State of Qin, who took flight to the west.

Those silken threads that hem the bamboo curtain within the Babylonian veil, to drain barbarians; for such secrets give the holder advantages; a head start, for there is a royal road to the arts and an art in supposing causes and moments.

The Zhou Dynasty universe was a cyclical function of weeks, withheld and scaled from the weak by the cutting and a knowledge passed on from descendant to descendant.

For this was the job of flow after the female characters left, especially one squaring the earth and boxing the gateways and mouths.

This was the Thing, the crossing, the promise to thrive and to prosper, by a confusion in politics, and so began the plot by those willing to change the crop [of words], and thereby the leaves of embarrassment and such is the source of the disease from which the Lu never rose.

For if the Thing was the night, the stars would be rotten. And thereby the ancient kings of heaven's creation became the source of tomorrow's ghosts of hate in order to win the world of benefits in addition to a world of harm by the manipulation of words.

An anger to be mastered by such a crossing division and this was placed in a book of songs where the small were thereby sacrificed in this crossing dance, and a plot that scattered prophets [profits] and decrees.

The country became happy with the benefits because political interests were at heart and by such orchestration, respect for teachers of the Li School with the keys.

For those who did not know of the Thing, its arts and music were those who could not learn, and could not make accomplishments, because they took no delight in learning [as they could not afford the payments, and they were ignorant, as they knew not what to learn]. And thereby political power was invented, division by knowledge, and also the appreciation of the mysterious.

For such was now the nature of the critical interpretation of words, the perhaps cut, and the meanings and spin by the line of justice. [And thus, the Pentagon was set for fresh washing in the towns] and such is the nature of those common people that were left behind, not knowing what day it was, nor of seasons of wind and rain, by such assertions.

And this is the fifty [ordering], five [elements] and the bone of contention. And so, laws were made for the Lu by the musical notes of Zhi, and the voices to note, and the beginning of the age of twelve, whereby such cutting became the Penal Code of the Lu. Thereby imprisoning them by such methods in the prostitution of critical reasoning and thereby Dogmatic was set [Dog-Ma], and the disobedient became a flock of sheep that became inevitable by the divisions and the beams in full swing and subversion.

Whereby the Lu moved the Empress from the garden by orders of such orchestration, and thereby this music became a hit for the Lu, unaware that the Books of Zhou were a light for the Houses of Lu.

For it was now as if the Lu were people, all with wrong-shaped teeth, yet they knew not that their new teeth had come from our military dentists depending on their retreat. And, that in time, the Lu would become as if mice without a tooth in their skulls.

For such was the nature of the serrated molars of our military dentists who serve society by the mouth, apprehending what the mouth should relish.

Yet the Lu were blind and unable to penetrate the mysteries of the music masters as they could not chew the words by their crooked teeth that we gave them. To taste the flavours making their mouths different and all alike, yet prone to the words of kings, to whom their teeth released a yes from some, and they became the Lu Ya Department, the yes men, and separate from the rest.

And such was the music for the song of the many who followed such regulations in great abundance; thus corrupted, we turned them around. And many put confidence in this subordination to the few at the top as special people of ceremony. All because of the special poetry and this dentistry.

Thus, the ancient reason to place the Ten Commandments at the top and the crooked mouths at the bottom; singing to the leaves and the radical rap words that hide meanings.

Whereby the belligerent win without casting a spear, and the vanquished are happy with the outcome and bowing in such submissive subjugation. Singing the text in the flow of the song blissfully unaware of what has been cut nor the nature of their losses and thereby carry on unable to hear the smell, nor knowing of the fan.

Brightness was to know the day in March [the first day of the year], and the march of the way, and the way of the dagger, as if the sun and moon in clarity, brilliant and clear. That the east is bright and of whom the court is crowded with the common people below disadvantaged and quiet, neglected by Li. Yet not daring to jump nor enter, nor examine the patterns that this stuff was made of.

For in the chaos, the Lu were ill-disciplined and a rabble of chattering crooked teeth. Yet by the Lu, there was no investigation as to the truth, nor any interest in the suspects.

For the Lu knew not distinguishing between the in between and not so; nor the rules of order and chaos, and how to make clear the similar and different.

For the Lu were indifferent, conquered by the ancient word cloud that flew well above Lu heads.

Imprisoned in political punishment, unaware of the principles of government and the implications of legal sanctions.

And so, to know was to rule in a world of gentlemen of private speech, yet acting as if they know nothing of their crimes, nor willing to teach of the lines that confuse the mastery of intentions in the formula to abuse.

For the gentlemen had no fear of heaven for they knew exactly what it was. For heaven was an affinity their parents enjoyed and so welcomed and perpetuated with accord. Whereby the people are held hostage by the light of the sun for the Lu know not the Light of the Moon.

This is the brightness of our implementation by the light of the moon that the hostages know nothing of.

Thereby the son of Adam and Eve was Set, a foundation for transacting business faithfully.

Set in place by those who are not faithful at all over a body of people without the keys to know and thus a congregation of those who cannot conceive the progeny of the words.

Thus brighten is abstaining from all of the Lu words.

For we are perpetuating this formula and method and all such regulations and details, and this is the good work. Where the language is a dagger of dogma, and truth is by us, and this method self-appointed.

Yet, I write for whom it is now time to see by moonlight.

Brightness is to be sovereign and a ruler of yourself. To be you; to know of the powers and the gateways, and of the bitter cuts.

To be good and able; wise to the Word Cloud above the Robinson and the lying ministers and their pull and pits, the defences and the cover-up on money.

With the will, measure and understanding of what is good, the light and the jam of the future; and the knowledge of those men who creep around only raising dust about yourself.

For this is a business to encompass and can; and enslaves odd men of talent in rivalry; for the even can.

The even encompass and thereby endure.

By means of order and timely opportunities where all things are a performance of the music, and money, profit and concealments, and a lack of attention to fitting words with frankness enabled for the expression of verity, intentions and accord. And such is the music to hear with your own eyes. For there are sorrowful hearts for those not taught clearly.

And so the superior go up.

Wisdom is to know the branches of knowledge cut off from the Wood that just bark like sleeping dogs. That is what you need to know. Knowledge is asleep for the many because of the Music Master Zhi and the higher branches to know and the nature of the hostages of the sun [consider sun from the ancient Egyptian meaning: to make an opening, to force open, the cause of; fish, arrow; to destroy, the large pool; to suffer pain, to be ill; and sun-t [or "qi"] the art of the physician, the science of medicine]; and this business of the furnace of flowing gold, of silk and cotton.

For the Lu are handled by being governed.

By ignorance to the gates of knowledge and the spaces in between. That the Lu are as if stretched leather; subordination drummed in them, and not looking for the call to the Black Mountain, resisting the open mouth to the cave, and they in proud temper stuck in the marsh at the foothills. Unable to take the old ancient classic of the opposite generation and rare, and separate one from the other, the meat and the bones that were scratched by sharp things as conjunctions.

By those who descended from those who made the ancient cut of the moonlight, making the Lu sole [soul] hostages of the sun [son].

As if in a cave where there is a rolling stone across, preventing the women entry to tend to the dead inside and unaware of the second at the higher level, or shunning such suggestions.

Most certainly required to peel the barbarians by trials in such nourishment.

For the rolling stone across is a sign for what was made in this fix of the crucial fiction that covered up by moonlight.

From the thick and many who'd had their branches cut off, and all they were left with was their bark; dogs as they known.

Power is achievement; engineering workers by force, as if tendons to shape the people. And such a good result.

Like this, we made them into our soldiers by our cunning creation in a science of crown and altered, and altars, riddling divisions, and haltered. This is a method loved by the Lu.

For we integrated this process with Lu rituals in ceremonies and music of birth, coming of age, and in marriage embedded, and death in a manner that the Lu never questioned.

For to the Lu, the music resembled the nature of heaven and earth by the penetrating virtues of our spiritual intelligences. And so we brought down the Lu spirits from above, giving the Lu a substantial structure in the subtlest manner of the duties between Father and son, and thereby we ruled the Lu as subjects. Thus the condensate of the word cloud was the fine body of the text, the collar of the Father, and the son [sun, child, gold] of this festival we won from the Lu sacrifice. By this crossing exchange a world of benefits, and by such verses a world of harm for the Lu and their disaster.

And by such death to the Lu souls we were inside their camps with this ingenious mysterious disease.

For in time they closed down their courtrooms [basilica] and made them their churches. And in those churches they sang our songs, to our music as a lament to our powers of creation and lyric to the spirit of our ink.

Thus an invitation and report on the child chapters and the western lid on the sacred feminine as the Lu sacrifice for war.

Our promise of their falling by poetry and the bone of contention for in them thereby we invented a want and cut the wood and built a wooden clotheshorse; an Iliad of chaos for the sunburnt leather [for those without hair] of the west. Who lost the girl to the east, and gained a selfish maniac hero as a war god who the Lu worshipped in war ships.

By Three, for three is the one and the two.

As words became our soldiers. And these bitter words made The Disease.

The Lord of The Lines. The Body of The Text

And, The Spirit of Our Ink. The Troy, the Three.

For such was our forefathers' art in heaven.

And these soldiers became our army, and by leaves and quills our defences.

By the language conquering the wood and placing them in suffering. For in time the pieces of their royal songs had found all their proper places by our craft of rearrangement and elemental ordering.

Re-mixed, they became the rock show of the empty skulls of Lu and the rolling stone across. For this was certainly an achievement in advance of any other art.

Relying on the heart of the temple to stop a city, stayed to idle. For by such a temple we have the measure of the earthly inch by inch. And now the Lu give us testimony by confession as if in court, and so by temple winds we win with their heart in our hands, now we have cut from them their intelligence and souls by such invasion of their inner walls.

And then we made things happen all by the strings and weaving of the classical Acts of Songs. For now, weighing heavy was our influence!

The Common Army is thus the lid on this vehicle for these fish. The ancient cloth, covering up this business, the wild penning of the barbarians that has made the need for fighting redundant with swords and spears, by our radical cover and this cross bar for yoking.

All by the language of assistance, we have developed the channels for draining barbarian juice by the shredding and cutting of wood, and ranking inflammation by the disease, and these we call the forming tendons of our network.

By relying on the heart of the temple and the smell of the currency of wealthy people for whom the music plays.

And by our music we hit back, and at times shock, with a bitter strike by the notes rolling as if punches in our hands, and of course, the ancient dagger.

For the Ancient Dagger is the sign of our inner city, which like the Word Cloud cannot be seen of what only the few conceived. Thus by this manner, we control cities as if they are our castle. All by the earthen ware pottery of our own creation, to which we've blown life into.

By the language of assistance, we create wants and desires to engineer the people by wrapped words in an attack the Lu do not fully understand; and for which, in any case, there is no mechanism for the many to securing accountability.

Thus by the assistance of language, we ensure the Valley of Lu have less by their lack of knowledge that we keep the bamboo lid on, that they owe and thereby we kill them by crafty clipping and reducing. Slaughtered like Greeks by our government control and nurture; by ranking and grading them, by telling they are all equals and by making them wait. All by the old weapon of the Ancient Dagger.

By stripping them of their will is a must.

We hide the radical cow, gave them the four elements and hide the other four, thereby denying them access to the elemental Eights that we cloaked in Mystery, Amen. Thereby we cut their full branches of understanding oratory, literature and reasoning, and this made them somewhat crazy in the mind, and thereby drained their souls as both a defence and a protection for our future and what is good for us by such sunlight and rhymes, and thereby the jam, for we made the Lu amenable.

By placing the lid over the measure of Sin-Cotton in this tangle, we created sleepy warehouses and manpower in our capture.

All by our will and measure for what is best for our futures and what was the nature of the sacrifice of the Lu to the Gods of War.

Yet we admit it was improper and unorthodox what we did in this work of the bone of contention by cunning engineering. Setting the Lu to labour by the commencement of one above in notes from the radical two. Thereby setting the shade cloud over the west for a long time and this we called righteous for them.

And so they paid respect to those words from our Ministry of Words, who inserted themselves between, and reordered their, ancient words and rituals, and that is how we entered their camps. By the word cloud that shades the sun, and this created beggars at the bottom of the Valley of Lu. By our wrapped words by which the Lu perish to a living dead by this destruction of their people, without the Lu realising that our ancient dagger had taken them hostage. Beggars that the Lu now were. Hee Hee. Thirsty, terrified, exposed by their ignorance to reason, and thereby, confused.

Far from them, the golden gates to the citadel would only open to horse people with the language of assistance as the keys.

Those with the rule book and a tongue with two strokes living amongst their people, as if a lynx rounding the ceremony song of this ceremony, yet they would be sparse those horsemen.

For the Lu were to be the last to know of the health and compassion of the nurse on Lushan [the cave on Black

Mountain] and what she implemented and the words that were changed.

Thereby from then on, the Lu knew only of a surname [sir name] and no longer of her guiding principles.

Unknown to the Lu, she remained in a palace high enough to observe the propriety of the sexes. Yet, she had been made the villain; and so only men ruled and this the Lu accepted, and so the Lu no longer drank of the night and knew not of the reality of her clothes' horse; for girls were just rambling about, and it became considered vain for the Lu to solicit them, and so the Lu became as if dead without this woman. As if perishing together on the dusty road by an ancient blade that was used to strip the young trees of their leaves, thus leaving their bark.

Thereby the Lu were not to meet the mouth [the gateway] of the evening, and knew not of rank, position and words with a smell like a spirit of ink, and a name, and made no tribute to her, nor her books, and thereby were unable to solve the Mystery by the gateways that opened after sunset.

And so the Lu became a people that knew only by the sun and were commanded by our Word Cloud that they did not know nor understand, and this cloud cover was their shade, and this shady cloud the Lu called their Lord.

Impeding themselves from the gateways to the elemental arts of Fives, and thus, the Lu became thick mouthed and doubting, incomplete within themselves by the spaces that lie in between the doors that were left open for the hostages of only the sun, much to the satisfaction of our small, three-legged table.

And so the sun did not leak a word from its mouth about this mystery. Yet for the small table, the sun and the moon were both clear and well. And so each morning at sunrise, from the east, the Lu made a ceremony of this sacrifice of justice, by the acknowledgement of the brightness from the East.

For the hostages of the son could not rhyme nor reason nor pivot any doors.

Their trials began with such rudeness, and they were peeled as required in such certainty of words, cored apart but made to feel special, also because their will by this method became easy to shape.

Thus, a cable of rules, laws and demands was winded around the Lu to inquire and extract their juice.

As if a rotten rope that squeezed the Lu whereby interpretation and questioning transformed to fear. That in the hands of the Lu people became the instrument of joy, and jealousy tensioned responsibly and thereby making wheat, grains and gain for us; for we had cut off their ears and taken their profits by setting their prophets and thereby draining them of Qi.

For the crossbow of the mouths are but darts from the gateways, and this is knowledge to know.

For there is a will to peel with this rotten rope, and an enemy we stalk in-between by wrapped words that keep returning from the space in between us and the Lu, for the ancient reason.

Because of [and due to the Department of Imports], the bleeding, the smoke, wisdom and Lee [Li]. Our official function by the Department of the Knife and our benefit from the western provinces that by such art and craft we force and is thereby our sharpness of merit.

For we never tire of eating more wealth and goods in this superabundance of property and wealth that we are draining from the Lu, to the extent that words are inadequate to explain.

For this is the measure of our ancient dagger and the nature of Lu homes by our rulebook and the horse that has breached their city walls of which amazingly the Lu accept.

For the ancient reason is the opposite of what the Lu understand and are the parts tucked in between the withering songs that can.

Whereby we have packaged goods that we acquire and in return we have sent them our ambassador, as a well-measured classic from the Word Cloud as the Son [of this great mystery to them] for we have become fond of stirring up confusion for the Lu, what with us now holding their horses.

Reason; due to our trading in such bleeding and smoke, we have placed the Lu alive in their coffins thus protecting our trade and our borders. Yes, indeed, and yet, the Lu have no knowledge of this art, for the Lu cannot comprehend such a craft.

Therefore, the ancient twilight was concealed by the helpful wrapped words from the people of the country of Lu, such incense, and the spaces between became the source of the ancient aftermath.

That once inside, we became satisfied in those spaces in between the folk characters as if garnering epilepsy and separating the Lu, that we felt was appropriate enough to wither by the bone of contention and thereby obtain and acquire to our satisfaction and just reward, and in return sending our messenger from the sun as our ambassador.

For to follow our ambassador brought sickness for the Lu, and fruits for us.

Yes, this covered the Lu in sweat through poetry that was too long, that fits to the times, and was willing to do the job. Increasing the tone of what was right and reasonable for seekers of truths from ancient facts not of today.

In those lines of deep words, to which the Lu duly agreed, the Lu could be tolerated by instilling a new behaviour to which there was no objection in advance. That only we profit from our map of the Word Cloud.

We called this the Mystery and its effect was the Disease.

Yet the knowledge was theirs for those with eyes that see.

Thus the ancient reason of the bone of contention gave the Lu the purpose of the dead, in which no one knows the truth, and thereby we planted expectations, placed the rolling stone across and created a rock show in their empty skulls by this interest in dead.

All by inserting our dagger between two periods of time that are connected to their place and therefore related to their lives. Parting the Lu houses from the dusty lane [the way] and in return granting the Lu the smallest room to use as a quantifier, an ancient measure. Causing the Lu to be separated and broken from black and white. Provoking the Lu by do not. And by do not, some Lu became our spies of righteousness, some of whom became seedlings that if we removed the dagger from their skulls might participate in "the meat, who seek, and those who want it". For such is the nature of the in-between interpretations [and the word "cloud and shade"].

For in the words we gave them the lines to work people and time, yet they see a difficulty, but not too much. For the Lu had to recognise learning, and become. For we pound the Lu. A processing government; and a world that laughs, yet stressed and annoyed, that by such rhetoric the enemy is not yet fully destroyed by just a surname.

Yet a country to die, without a head for what? Of the right side of the road, and help and care from Tigers that are there.

Deceitful liars that they are, we hiding [their] conceit; the key to the words of madness of the disease. Lies and words that bully, that perhaps one day the Lu might have a birthday [initiate], that the Lu might read without deceit and illuminate the fraud of such beliefs that cheat with such ceremony of the conceit from the Black Mountain cave.

That the Lu might see with open eyes the nature of society in all phenomenon and activities, fall in love with situations and make those pieces an industry of change.

That the Lu might reason the occurrences and calamities, work for the casualties, and bring an end to the disease. To change their occupation in relationship to responsibility for knowing of The Thing, the rules and service of the Lu children of this matter in this business that is no accident.

This matter that the Lu have allowed became a king above their heads without thinking for what it is worth, nor the expenses, nor the sadness and weeping; nor the suitability. Unaware it has made them dry of juice that required their very own effort to dry. They now, as if stressed fish, turn but all the same, and we as if dolphins and stranglers by golden ground pharmacy.

Yet who of the Lu have seen this?

Do they know to what song they agreed?

That this ambassador has forced their service for money, who sent away the lady of life by false cause and devious premise, and ordered the Lu to work?

Reporting to others and by workers' poison and angled crossbars that are now our chopsticks.

Persuading the Lu to run in circles phased by a lack of knowledge and commandments.

Reporting to our judicial organs to administrate complaints and thereby penned and under our control.

Announcing each situation as it arises, exhausted by what to do and all sold out.

Yet unaware we hold more stocks of poison at the Ministry of Reports and newspapers to accuse and sue.

This enemy we've befriended, for whom all rights have been reserved, for the widowed public by the hand of Horse [Ma] anger, in this conflict of interests that cannot be compatible without the special light of "Gé". The old bone of contention and oldest known conspiracy in this art for war and one-sided understanding.

For this reason are the bones of the anatomy of man. The reason of the reason, and thus because, the fruit and sickness, the following delays, the covering of the sweat that is the juice indeed, and the wisdom of necessity for the recovery of the ears as elegant conjunctions for the adverbial, with the vocabulary of the table of the Word Cloud in hypothesis.

For such is a knowledge that many do not know, for there is a small table and rose.

And therefore, a quantification of the unexpected things. Where for the Lu, change had become a barrier. For cause was not a marginal thing. Cause was the origin of the Thing. Cause determined and killed. An intentional murder and knowing before that was guilty.

And all the old things, the peoples, their soil and their homes, their motherland, and piles of papers were discarded. All for the sunburnt without hair, our banks, auction houses and keen interest.

Getting rid of the old for the establishment of the new. Setting a dance to self-styled original steps that were not of Lu creation, but of Lu restrictions. Then sealed as the status quo, not for progress but that we might rest on our laurels and friendships in this funeral ceremony for the Lu by our prophets.

And so, the talk is the laugh of the wind, public mourning and the meaning of life, a few dollars, and hard attitudes, swallowed until it hurts, and that is the disease.

Yet for people who have learned, there is a door and medicine and causes in the ancient words of old, and of sun and moon and transliteration.

That will let you spy on us. From the remote path on Black Mountain that few seldom ever beat to seek an ancestral meet.

In an elegant assembly of wooden bars like a shelter is this quiet court of nobility in rhetoric, Can and ancient medicine to follow.

That is in service of the force of money and causes all things false. [For the wooden bar are the beams of the lady].

The Lady of Such As, who you should follow with obedience for she is the Doctor, yet she'll nurse and show you how to weave.

In periods of time, and she knows the limits to learning, the quantifiers, what can be published and what is better left unsaid.

For she is not seeking recklessness nor death.

For she is giving out fives as if elementary banknotes, as if documents used for underwriting, and undermining generations by elements unknown.

Gold. Wood. Water. Fire. Earth.

Mountains of study, healthy life sciences and powerful creations.

And this we called the musical score of the conflict.

All of which is hidden in between.

And this is the foundation of the Thing.

So, just deny this and say there is nothing to do!

So, the Lord or Lady is the owner of these powers. Of which it is my intention to wright for you.

Traditionally, the old courtiers of the king, had the special look – the correct view on how to deal with policy decisions and the power to decide for the people from what was most important to most basic. And this we call the Imperial Force. The Will.

Well, the morning sun and rain.

All based on a set of ancient understanding of the Horse [the Ma]. The wooden framework and the rose [rows].

Where to know is to have passed the ancient test, where there is hospitality for guests of "know of" who understand each other, good people who become old friends. Of which is wisdom.

Knowledge of the indispensable need and in health, home, aspects, essences and things to content to contend and decide, connect and correct. And man-made things. And this we call the farming.

The special look over the wild world, the stresses and how to escape by becoming healthy, teaching, learning on the ground, volunteering, asking the blind, leading the people, forming tables of comparisons and limiting levels and matters connected to banks.

To thereby guard the future.

To become a Yu.

Which is a You, without an empty circle.

To learn to see all things from the opposite perspective. To flip upside down. To see two aspects of experience. By using the enemy's spies to create contradictions and feed the Lu the suitable.

Creating, when necessary, boycotts, betrayals or resistance to the local establishment.

Fighting back and thinking for yourself by your own judgement, purely by your ability to ask yourself and to trust your own judgement. This is the anti [the counter, the opposite], the fat auntie of the ancient meat – for your ancient calligraphy needs to become greasy.

All of which knowledge lies in between what the Lu know and what we do in our misdirecting.

Therefore, the original barriers Can change for the Lu. The disease – can change. The tripod [banks] can change. Our restrictions can change for the Lu.

By looking at the fat auntie [the ancient reverse in the in verses], thinking and asking yourself what lies in between [and the hidden meanings – for we changed the meanings as we like spicy too, and clever people].

Otherwise [I do not know] the purpose of those ancient kings and I do not know hope, sincerity and tolerance and such are things not [knot] to know. And thus I do not know, and now nor do you – for such are our policies that discriminate between the superior and inferior, and the obligatory nature of censorship.

§1.2

Therefore, unexpected things are of interest and capital generation and thereby military in nature and a function of the Thing.

The near and dear are the insiders at the palace, the people who can see and know about relationships.

The big who know of Twilight, and are thereby consistent in their conclusions by the self-organising logical efficiency in the currency of the profits.

Those with the right to see in between the reward that is bestowed by a tour of two books.

Pleasing to the eye, recognising human abilities, attention and a praise of knowledge. Noble words of light that draw a conclusion on Twilight, the desert of the majority and the thickness related to the spaces in between.

The Thing is the Twilight.

That which is dense and tight, sealed and clothed and set, and in full swing and secret. Not a thing to be open about. For The Thing is an agency machine, energy of words and purpose to explore in the spaces in between.

The not echo. That seems ridiculous to the unaware.

In the decorated text with which to become familiar and to learn.

The wisdom of the noblest people of the past.

The Emperor's arguments; the purpose of intelligence, and this is the highest achievement of knowledge.

The wisdom of the machine. Of insight, reason and perception.

The otherwise ability. The Force. The talent of the craftsman for the divisions. The Will. The Energy. What the ancients called the three-legged turtle.

Of which the secret is affordable, available as the food of the words to use in between, yet takes time.

Learn to change before the change with benevolence and righteousness otherwise the force goes bad in between.

Learn to change before change by the small things [the elements] that are hidden and thereby obscured.

Yet secretly visit them.

For they are wonderful and beautiful.

Kit Kat magic; and the Medicine for the sun.

Otherwise the ability.

Get it?

To look closely in between.

Tune up on the small details.

By the tables of logical reasoning. Who, what, when, where, why and how?

The cube for your observation of dimensions.

The elements and the carved integral lines in logical reasoning.

Know by the languages to doors and the tendons that form the households. Otherwise, use the spaces in between.

In between is the Thing. Not [knot] Hair, and thus the issue emits.

Yet previously, the smell was made known to the doors of the ears by those ancient persons in between.

As opposed to the doors and the tendons informing and reporting by those ancient persons all that everyone knew that was whispering.

Whispering about the dead: the loss of health and life, as if dead, and the chess that is played below the ground.

The Qi [sacrifice of life's determination] such as the death of a warrior in War.

The stubborn.

The Unconscious and all asleep.

Inactive and inflexible.

The Ancient Dagger.

The Lost texts.

The and Also, thus:

The Music.

§1.3

Therefore, use a look in between to have:

Cases of justice well prepared.

What belongs to whom? What occurred?

The manner in which the situation changed?

What is estimated or by comparison?

Knowledge of what is said?

Good manners.

And Also, the music by the elements.

To have life in the city, the countryside and as a gentlemen or lady, and all in between.

To have health as an insider.

In between, to have the front to use all of the opposites in between.

To have the measure of the wooden case of justice [that is the coffin of our creation for the masses] about the dead. Their loss of health and life, that makes them as if the dead; and the chess-like strategy that is played from below the ground.

To know the nature of the sacrifice of life's determination as if the death of a warrior in war and of:

- The Stubborn.
- The Unconscious and Asleep.

- The Inactive and inflexible.
- The Ancient Dagger.
- The Lost Texts.
- The Bird Screams.
- The Music.
- And having the insight of all things in between – the uncooked rice.

Granting you the song of an idea of what must be missing from the common understanding of the classical books by comparison and the efforts of thinking by such insights.

For this is the Party Method, the festival and the well-framed Case of Justice for the dead.

For it is only for the well prepared to get to see what belongs in the ancient books. That is, what occurred with the disease.

The situation to change, the method to change by estimation and comparison of truth, clarity and detailed observations.

The knowledge, the etiquette, the music and also.

To gain health is as if a birthday; to be reborn refreshed to the ancient knowledge.

To know matters that are of the production of the machine [the instrument].

The nature of the death of those still alive and the mourning public.

How to maintain a prosperous life for yourself.

The disease, the gas, the effect, the flower strokes and the talk of the laughing wind.

How to make the fuel burn up – the fire.

The immature melons.

The uncooked rice and the juice.

The sparse, the guest, the word, the street – and those not familiar with the uncommon.

The unskilled, the hand, the untreated iron, the hard, the swallowed. The deep and the fear [that] hurts.

For people who are learning the doors are people who have knowledge and know the intentional confusion [of Confucianism], the Medicine and the traditional role for the small to play and are good at resting and thereby Healthy with such knowledge of what lies in between.

For knowing Between is to be freed by the interpretation of the word cloud network from the shackles that bind the simplified.

To have leisure is to be free from simplified characters, and such is the interest of the word cloud.

Thus between is to know periods of time that connect two things and their relationships.

Between is also a creation space or time we can call a field or people. Also, the part of the house going into a room. A lane. The coat. The amount of. A quantifier, a measure; a while, an instant or recently. A gap. Children. Without intimacy, separated, unconnected.

To get it; daybreak to the black-and-white phases, without provoking people. Spying on the anti-figures and forms. And the removing.

The remote path, from the path. Meat for those who seek it, and want.

Whereby in such matters and manner, Between becomes a big thing that few know of for such reasons as oaths to secrecy [implied and required] in initiation.

All of which knowledge grants a freedom from the shackles of the simplified characters.

Whereby the insights of the elements become outstanding and unfold as your passport to the ancient source of the whispering grass that the branchless trees – those stumped – don't need to know; the music department of sound, colour and Li.

By lying, that which is a night-time activity. From which one obtains classified energies, colour generation, from where there is a code to get to the source by a set of invisible standards. For such actions are to begin singing and to find the Thing.

For the Lu, trees cannot be allowed to know the wisdom of the times and of these ancient roads and blades.

For such matters are the realms of the wonderful illumination that flowers in bloom, known as the twilight. That you might blossom without blemish.

For with one it is impossible to draw a consistent conclusion. In which Love can help. For love requires two. Therefore, all you need is love. [Two and thus progeny].

To know this is to pass [from living dead to life], to be clear on the road and the blade and the ayn [causes] of the rand [the leather], the names to express feelings and time. The Good, the difficult to enter and darling – for she has exquisite beauty.

For such is the knowledge of the old friends of ancient wisdom of the inexplicable tranquil and alone. The fruit. The instructions from the words that speak.

And, to be inside as an insider.

An insider means to be able to say with confidence that you only know one and can confirm you know nothing of two and to deny such existence too. For such is purely speculation.

And in this manner you must play along if you are happy to eat Li food of the ancient dynasties.

Hence, in this manner, such secret notions are dismissed by all academic establishments and people in power as a speculation, in exhortation, whereby denial is but a rouse by tricky people who know too, seeking perpetuation, or confused wooden barking from the House of Lu.

For such is the nature of interpretation from the word cloud.

And so believe in the ancient silken words the ancestors carved on the bones of ancient meat from the place where the sun and moon meet, the Source, the Well, the Zion.

For those characters explain and classify the workers by recognition and said through poetry and time by the language of assistance to the subject to be stated, and the logic of the sentence composed.

For such are indeed real means for seekers of truth from facts.

The true Zion and the disciplines.

And to learn of the silken yarns already there, and so learn about yourself.

For there is such a thing as machine calculation by the mind, based on the primordial elements, developed from the elements that we call the Eights. For the Lu know no more than seven, the celestial elegancies for Lu conduct and good behaviour, by our Imperial decree.

That in time, [whilst a great secret] you may discover something especially surprising and induce a greater synoptic clarity and speed of mind by such connections. For by effort and attention by delineation and recall there is an inheritance from the ancestors that can be accessed and unlocked from deep within the subconscious mind, and the day of such occurrence will be your birthday too.

Whereas the Lu are confused to this notion of cognition, and by false reasoning, the Lu accept our dagger in their skulls, making them a superstitious people. Who now worship people after they are dead, considering them immortal. Whilst in more recent times, the Lu believe in a wizard who became an immortal, and for them this has become their crucial fiction, whereby it is as if their souls are turned upside down.

Yet no one else can teach you of such things.

You must learn alone from books of the feminine discipline in between. Remembering the way, the blade, the chaos, the leather and the silk, and then find those scattered silken threads, then link this to cotton onto the amenable transliteration.

From the benevolent noble men of talent in this ancient business of letters from the mausoleums of emperors, princes and pharaohs of good conduct and respect; and thereby learn about You from their mouths, the word cloud and their treasures.

For the ordinary people are but apes evolved by the use of tools and can use the language of communication only as animals.

The second types are others who know of the blade and the fish and the sun, and act sincere; yet use the manipulating blade.

The third are of a human quality now almost lost with a temperament and reputation that cannot be understood by those who lost the texts for this ancient business; and in such noble respects lies the treasure at the apex, our humanity and times.

For the treasure can be the jade. Our defences. The Ancient Dagger. The country. Jane. The Emperor's letter. The king's speech, where to Break is to call the temple word, and to Call is to enter the market forearmed with the insights of the ancient country and the people for your contemplation. And, of the [unseen] opportunities in the market place, side by side with qualified perspectives of the times.

[Because Reason is the Vitruvian Man by Da Vinci.]

The objective insights of causes and effects between people, their communities, their states and their counties for your consideration and application.

To know before the event conditions of what is likely to follow and what is likely to drag. For fruits, the disease, and the Also – and this is the mastery of the people with the special look.

To thereby import fire to any given situation of Because; in the markets in respect to the apes, the others and the humane. By the recovery of your ears and opening of your eyes, to see the rose of the table from top to bottom, thereby the natural igniting of your mind.

Seeing the heart of all functions, the goods available, the words and the profits, the costs, the effects and the talents, the This and so forth; together as a function of use.

And this is the Call reason, and this is the Also.

And, thereby the scientific capacity to spy on the inside of such places, people, good fortune, calamities and schemes of men.

From the inside, is to know the related external perspectives on the ground, in Court and on the line. The feminine. And, the villains.

And once ordered and satisfied to accept income by those who, all by the contemplation of the political men and by learning how to use them, and how they use others, by such careful detailed observation, reason and consideration.

That can only happen by those who know if, if. And all things in such a perceptive speculation and engagement.

For which there are the cavities in government, those with a station identified by our intentions, and those with a hall and our desires. The conditions of our houses. And, the device of the elements, the three types of people, the tables, the ears, the subjects and the predicates, the modification and thereby the connections with the functions of Use and the eyes by engagement and resolution to our well-planned eventuation.

To turn the Lu around, by our way of well-ordered thinking by first-hand experience by:

- Making things complex, such as turning things upside down
- Introducing side deals
- Reversing and creating contradictions
- Resisting

- Developing premonitions about what you know is about to happen
- Refuting
- Expounding analogies

All of which will confuse the Lu further, and by this process you will learn more, by keeping the Lu happy, relaxed and talking freely to you as the subordinating superstitious wild yappers they are.

Because this method is to gain an insight of our enemy by the contemplation of our enemy from the inside, and employing what we learn that they give to us freely.

For like words, these characters who are our enemy will have gaps in between. That if gently wedged open, out will flutter short-tailed birds of great interest from their tongues. Thus allowing us to use our in between procedures.

The contemplation of that will bring about Lu deaths by the following eight categories:

1. As a punishment and ill health for the relatives of those already dead and are now thereby our prisoners
2. By Qi that they sacrifice life's determination, thereby death of the warrior within them
3. By creating stresses for the stubborn and shock, and hard sells that they might have a heart attack
4. That we send them to sleep
5. That we tie them in knots, and thereby bind them and make them inactive, for by the ties that bind them they collectively subordinate
6. The Ancient Dagger and the leather in their texts
7. By the Music and musicians and gymnasts
8. The Bamboo Horse Whip [the skilful negative use of the Mystery to psychologically direct and undermine inferior people by limiting critical reasoning, inducting chaos in human situations and in matters of heart mind and soul. Whereby the uncertainty of understanding – in knowing there is a mystery that they do not understand – creates an internal self-conflict and thus a lack of confidence in the self – that at the subconscious level

preoccupies those who do not understand; being the well-ordered orchestration of all of the above]

For all are means to bring about Lu deaths, or that the Lu might live, but be as almost dead, by having their Lu minds annihilated by us wiping the necks of those sheep whose blood they have donated to us in exchange for our blunt dagger.

And such is to be the construct of Lu government and judiciary and opportunity. The Lu are to be deluded, lied to, cheated and deceived. In their duties, careers, in pursuit of their engagements, in their service and all things, and this false logic of mad words they do not realise has to be the process for all foreign countries and conditions that we might drain them of their juice.

Thereby we can by use of the Thing that we by elemental word intelligence shake Lu currency and therefore profit with the lies of words of heaven, by the thing and straight hook of wrapped words in twos the Lu carry as a deception for the deceived and are deluded by our framing device.

For we will let credit and auction houses be our teacher.

And thereby grind the Lu in a learning.

For which the Lu volunteer.

As if we asked the blind for what we take from Lu people by our tables.

And thus limit the Lu by levels with a guard for the sparse. Whereby Lu belongings become our future juice. All by traditional drama based on the old novel where the Lu end up in our net as unsung heroes.

Confused by markets in crisis. Deceived by The Thing.

Their belongings are our future.

We with net, auction house, and patient.

For Summer Dogs of War are foreign, ill and unaware. And staggeringly mistaken.

And thereby imperial, such decrees defend us by such perceptions, recognition and knowledge, whereby we gain control through engagement and well-ordered resolution, by eventuation to our desires.

For the Lu also let us know, by Make, the ancient fox we set amongst them, and the smell of each Lu reputation.

The old fox Make can also make the Lu excited with printed words too, and so we can hear about all respects, of church, and the nobility.

And getting the Lu excited more, we hear of what the Lu Love, and they even tell us of their dreams.

By which we use those words to keep the Lu small, between the reporting of their knowledge as if sheep with chattering teeth that the Lu can be.

By the promulgation to our enemies of words they do not know as if a gift to those children by our Code Book that they call a canon, that is by a crooked song of said, of crafty eights, to mill their wheat.

What in reality is a summons to our courts, suing their minds, for prosecution by the persecution of a crucial crossing fiction for their juice.

And so this knowledge of our enemy [for whom all rights have been reserved] is a further pass within the ancient test.

All of which is based on lifetimes of assessments and can be seen by the [mental] health between the people.

That we can turn them over, by what they report to us, the goods they supply and by controlling their newspapers [and channels of media].

All by thinking and asking ourselves in the opposite perspective to what the Lu know, from the cover of our small table.

And so we invented a counter to report.

§1.4

Sunshine – For the Sun's [Son's] Only [Child] Said.

For to know is to be aware that the Sun, from ancient oriental times can also mean the outer branches at the end of the bamboo curtain, naturally regenerating the breeding of the descendants of the sun. And times of old was also the interpretation of the coded network and the knotting, and thereby the method to escape by the times of less colour [by the respect of the light of the moon, and to know time; knowledge that the Lu did not have].

Child, can also mean the interest from gold, the fruits. The scholars and the boatmen. The teachers of morality. People who know of holes. Late at night. Chaos. Fat. And, in reading softly – knocking the two under the door.

Said, paired the word cloud and invented poetic forms as art. For Said is universally elemental: firstly water, secondly fire, thirdly wood, fourthly gold, fifthly soil. And this Said called the Music, the poetry or song.

Thus, what can also be interpreted from the above is the coded profitable network of the attribute holes in the music. For sun is the story of the Sun's only progeny, golden and illuminating.

And this is the nature of the Oriental nose disease. For the ancient plot restricts barbarians who do not understand the oriental language or that the symbols and their methods became, in the west the intellectual rules of art.

Where today perpetuation of this disease benefits the few. For the few who know of this and perpetuate, benefit by the conceit and a smugness of knowing something that others do not. And so, the disease is a teaching disease, allowing the many to die in ease. And such is the nature of the plot of the Oriental nasal [knowing] sickness of soft taking [whilst the many have their noses blocked up].

Where the Thing is the division of the many. Ground by such serrated teeth as if the mortar and pestle of a fine disunity, want more and couldn't care less. For such was colonisation, crown and altar and the power to subordinate creating the good, and those spies of the organisation to check up on each other and the many in the fine tuning of the music's tone and pitch.

And so the nature of the Thing has to begin with the conspiracy of meanings in a secret organisation that has become heaven on earth for the few who drain [towel and turban] the juice of the many.

Where the Thing depends on division. For such is the root and cause of crown and altar, and organisational hegemony.

For the Thing is the promise to be policed by the subordinating threat of embarrassment [or exile]. Orchestrated by the music, pressing Zhou Li by such a palm-less [handless] [woodless] method, where it is the palm that directs the changes to the crop, as if by the magic of a God, and thereby substantiated.

For it was the power of creation of the ancient kings that gave the people gods, and thus tomorrows ghosts in order to win in the world of benefits, as if by the condensate of a fine body, collar of the father and Son of this great festival. As such, ceremonies and music are the nature of heaven and earth [the word "cloud construct of prosperity"] and thereby the foundation established the Establishment.

Whereby those who do not take the effort to learn are either told by family or friends [the near and dear] or simply cannot delight in such learning.

Because with the Thing, all rights are reserved.

For the thing is the crossing [the Xing – to thrive, prosper and flourish – and thus the promise for us to be], yet as if a double cross for the Lu.

For the work of the Thing is to learn and build, and thereby the creation of the waste to be. That is sending early to sleep, by night sleep sound. And, thereby the prevailing permission in the world for the dead for whom everyone is responsible in a great myth that we are all in life together and somehow there is a fairness, just some unfortunates, and calamities.

Yet, few stop to realise that the function of the Teacher is the function of division. For the teacher is all about conduct and the collective force to juice. Although of such and by this process few teachers fully understand this secret role that the organisation employs.

For Shi is the teacher, who is just as division. For Shi is the leader, the mental health, the medicine, the technology, the ancient laws, the fan, and thereby the collective force that grades and ranks the people by a form of intelligence that works for the organisation; yet not for every radical, and not in every situation. For such are numbers and probability that pen sheep by perceptions of conduct by commandment of the ancient kings' gods and this is Shi too for the many.

Out tax the many and swindle them for Li by the Ancient Dagger.

Where the out is the back-story of an opera of independent repertoire from the inside. Where the pliant subordinates are early to flock and happy with the cage.

Forcing the many to pay, in a cunning plan that ensures the many do not have enough. Whereby with intelligence and leaves, many can be tracked.

As can production, growth, goods and talents, occurrences and Things, revealed and extremes, from the vantage point of on the ground to hear citations, and see allusions, and look for more and their trends and effects, the mention and the problem.

For in such respects the levy is the ancient dagger, the husbands of other men, the people themselves, the fabric of the clothing, and the traveller's vessels.

The forces of the levy are the services, the discussing and this Old Bone of Contention – this war without combat, where the many have been recruited as soldiers. For that is a gathering of troops [the unaware] and the horses [those with noses for the smell].

Where the tax is the grain of the wood and the grain is the gain. The proof is the letters in their texts, and the revealing special signs.

For the levy is a sign of traditional characters. Symbolic in representation to our ancient force.

Where such ancient force is our organisation by horses [Caballa – the feminine form of caballus – the jade, packhorse, the old [useless] nag; see fish; cabala] of millions of words of such measures and metaphors to test, repeatedly the fine changes to the poem for the simplified characters by such autumn generation of coded signs and logical reasoning.

The many families must pay the fees for our defences, for school fee is to learn of Er in their defeat.

For this is the cost of the people.

This cost is their Sacrifice to the Gods of War. And their Sacrifice to the Gods of War is the cost for the Lu.

For the many are our banknotes. Commonly used as capital. Those made of steel, by our forging to steal by [organisational] generation, the [double] crossing and the Lu's subsequent resignation from life.

For the Lu, costs are their sacrifice to the war god of our creation.

For the Lu, money is as if flowers, in time it withers and dies; for the Lu know not time.

Yet with money, we are teaching the Lu of our power over them and the significance of the Lu sacrifice in this war. Thereby we have made money a teacher, and the costs of the lessons are payable fees.

Thereby the people of those families serve us and must offer their respects.

For we have made the people of the Lu selfless and with an integrity for everyone's interest. The Lu sees this as positive and thereby the Lu are big hearted despite having little by our design of the Word Cloud system.

Whereby this selfless integrity as a whole is a cunning social security network of the public. Everyone at the lower levels knows about each other and everyone is open and reporting and running to tell of others of all incidents, accidents, and affairs. And, by such manner, we can bag the Lu as livestock by our outside pens, as insiders of the family organisation.

In respect to families, there is the court, the dependents, the garden, the spectrum, the private schools, the city, the wind, the training and the Rules [such as with respect of the sensitivity of the number of Jane]. And, this is for old families, who can and have relatives and ancestors and are not wild.

Whereas the wild, are simple livestock. Poultry.

Farmers are people who operate an industry or have a certain identity, having mastered some kind of special knowledge, or are rich in practical experience.

The private schools deal with the confusing methods, the road and the blade [the Ancient Dagger] and the spirit of the ink in respect to the vertical and horizontal tables, the rose and the hundred duties, with, the quantifiers to make the calculations specific to the organisation.

All of which is in respect to the Wind. The Feng. The Bearing on the Many. That is respectfully holding hands, feasting, the offering and the worship to the Gods of War.

The Wind. That is the cardinal bearing many have to comply with, by the law abiding for the standard as a criterion and the line of the story according to the old rules. The Feng accompanies reports, accompanies persuasion and meets with gifts. The Wind is also the letters of faith and support for the ancient paternity. Thereby, overall the Wind is the salary from those sacrificing to the Gods of War; or perhaps, better stated an official income from the Lu salary that pays our pensions in gold.

Therefore, one can read the significance of the wind on the bearing of the Lu and the ease of process in respect to our effort as long as the music is harmonious.

The fee for each Hostage of the Sun for The Gods of War is a thousand swindled pieces of gold.

For the Homers were those we had the measure of.

The ancients used the shadow [the shade] of the sun to measure the time, and so the device of degrees of our organisation and measures [and also a sundial]. Thus the day and night classes were relative to light and darkness, and thereby censored.

By measurement of time, one could calculate the units to work and the benefits. Most of which the Hostages of the Sun, knew very little if at all.

Thus such fees were the Lu's sacrifices due to the Gods of War. The costs being the disappearance of Lu's money, the costs of consumption and the costs of learning; of which the latter was painstaking, yet the only solution to the evil of the Disease of the poetry was by such measures of gold.

Where gold belongs to the five elements, and also refers to the inscriptions of the Zhou, the instrument and is a weapon of war.

Inside, the Lu borders harass and agitate the Lu, create uncertainties and keep making changes; then from inside the inside scoop. For the Lu all end up in our net.

For this is the traditional drama for the Lu. The history of their history based on our narrative characters of the ancient novel.

To know of such things is another pass. To benefit from such things is to be a foreign businessman in the Valley of the Lu, and to know the edges, the causes and the line of the ancient dagger with our family in such provinces [the star people] and the Show.

The Show is the disruption, the creative instability and uncertainty. Thereby a worry for the Lu and their sadness that the frivolous Lu women lament from the ancient goods, the poetry and culture we gave them, the smell of [the spirit of] our urine and their sacrifice to the Gods of War.

For those who know the Sweep; that is, how to take a bamboo broom to the garbage on the ground, and dusty with insight to the switching crossing, the losses and the signs of sacrifice to the Gods of War that can move to action and move meanings, for such are acts of songs.

Giving energy to the static state and the relative, the chaos of method, the people chords of such capacity for oscillation of the strings.

Creating lazy in roads for our ancient daggers.

Those credited teachers of good health for the Lu. For the Lu tell us where to direct our ancient blades and the medicine that they will react consistently to the superstitions of our powerfully creative organisation as their sacrifice to the Gods of War, with the language of affections. The Lu children are thankful in apology in this way.

Let the road be for the Lu a passage of traffic for our due juice. Directing the Lu to a new way of thinking. For the Lu are raw.

Make profits, but do not start gymnastics with the Thing, thus do not speak of the Thing. For what the Lu has lost is to our benefit. Let the Lu wash in a bath with our measure [homer] of cold water.

Gymnastics are to get caught with the ancient dagger in your hand and being forced to make a correction. Just as gymnastics are to speak in the language of signs, to talk the opera of the word cloud. All in respect to the thing, by those who use ancient poetry to fan [the wind].

Do not speak of the thing.

The Qi of the Ten Commandments must penetrate the Lu homes and Lu families. The Lu must not learn above the seven celestial excellencies [thus not the eights and nines] of capital; thereby we restrain the wood. Nor talk of the source of the nine plus one; the Ancient Dagger; for the cross is the ancient dagger for the many who know not of the family system [of the households].

Phase the Lu defences and their fates year by year, and spend several years to dry each Lu generation in succession.

For phase means an interaction by the two sides. Such knowledge is the cross, mutual to those who know of the two.

The rows of the lines are the rose [the blooming illumination of the feminine] that handle the forces of movement for people in this field by doubling [signs] [in sets of two; coupling].

A square [fang] was in ancient times the wooden board used for writing; and also for writing medical prescriptions. The notion of the square also means direction; convention; standards, the method of the way of the pang, the universal. For the wood, the issues are persistently coming, whereas for the wind [those who know of the two] the phases are consistently repeating reciprocally by our order.

Thus, the bamboo measure is to wait patiently and rank and grade the gateways [the opportunities] together with the signs, our engagement and resolution.

The knowledge is to recognise and understand these things and to see the eventuation.

To pass is both to summons, and to propagate and transmit bamboo symbols.

Following is to continue and carry on between the doors [at the place, locale].

Shape is The Thing with form; that is the condition of the circumstances – that the forms create – and to know the punishments too.

Thus, by this method, one can start to sew and stitch deficiency. Get it [left foot upward as a sign] and to plunder beneficial [dishes] and profit from such advantages that become clear [in twos].

For by this method of reciprocal "fortune telling" by such coordination combined together, more becomes apparent in respect of the outside.

And so, the set of two of the universal square has been a long time in the office of government.

And so, the above can be the action of a party with a certain objective in the field that you will see personally from your nose [knowing] the names associated with the female health [such as the Princess Weeks], for her moon phases give us the four weeks of seven, and thirteen of her cycles in the community year.

Thus to phase is to give a child-like appearance to what is for us gold.

Surgery is to judge appearances by such observations and predict the probability of outcomes.

Auxiliary refers to an auxiliary person; ancient special refers to the highest official. The auxiliaries are to be slaughtered.

Alternating the flow of matters [the current] is an integral part of the flow. Thus, changes in the moments [of time][or a position, such as a situation] can be used to determine a state and this is called a phase, and knowing this is called the phase angle.

Because words generate the signs [images or forms] and therefore, two [as in a two person] can consider the words and thereby observe the images. When the images generate ideas in this method, two can contemplate the images and thereby observe the associated ideas.

All of which requires us to keep the lid on the measure of such matters in the following manner.

Taking care in maintaining the cause and the achievements of the predecessors; namely the royal, and secondly the body who love themselves to maintain their own sections; where the sections are consistent in their help and inking rules.

When in a place they cannot move, they strain the rabbit [the widow].

They comply with the laws and time; and do not change the status quo [Paul], due to the old reason.

They stay together and serve together.

The festival exercises are gymnastics, and leaning back gives juice. Whereby such Zhou Dynasty officials act as thorns [such as officials of the temple, as local government officials].

In respect to two numbers, these are the words that can be divided [from the other words] and calculated by the few, not the Hostages of the Sun. The skill is the ability to match, the small and also. And, fate is the gas of Li.

Thus one by one calculation does not work, only by twos. The nine two are more prominent. Blame is to enumerate the fault or fall. To talk or to tell is to forget the ancestors. The Lu have forgotten their original situation; and also have ignorance as to their own history.

In respect of the year, the earth goes around the sun every thirteen four-week moon phases at a time, and this knowledge must be further confused.

Ensuring every year will be a profitable salary.

The beginning of the year is a new section for Li.

The supplies of the year come from the ritual paintings, and supplies must be limited, and such is to be a deep secret for a long time.

The harvest is king, and the King [Li; profit] likes shortages. A year is hence also a discipline within the community. Whereby we constantly faze the wood, and such is the nature of the phasing.

To fight [in the old font] is to contend with the One alone against the hostages and is the best ever victory.

For we have created bitter music for the Lu Valley with the Ten. That we might take from them, pull and use them at our will. For Ten is a baseless assertion, and music to calm the Lu to stillness. Shun the Lu should they start to open and close the many doors of the material, because the Lu people waste words.

Do not be good to the Lu; keep the Lu sad and suffering.

In regard to time, maintain our sovereignty, prosperity and unity, and kill the Lu with calamity and adversity. This is the purpose of time for the Lu, and the classical orientation we have given the Lu, and thus the boundaries to the inside that we may become rich from the Lu.

For day and night, people are relative classes; thereby, we always win the day. For the Lu do not mind our benefits. For the Lu do not know they are in a struggle to defeat, nor that our intended purpose is Li, Get and Coupons of easy taking within a comfortable grasp. For we are over dominant of the Lu, yet the sleepy-headed Lu do not know. Therefore, we are kings of our environment shaping by the ancient woman's accessories and colours that we can bear the old read without any trouble; and for that the Lu are grateful. Yet the old read is not grateful to the Lu nor do the Lu cause trouble now for there is no sense in tense with the Lu.

And so love the jazz [the way we chew the music for the Lu yet they still enjoy our harmonics], and we receive from the Lu blessings in gold. For our love of gold coin grants a hundred golden coins that we take on the Lu's behalf. For such is the progressive table of the few. For we complement each other for the Lu are thick and not strong at connecting the adverbial and central vocabulary of our modification, such as "elusive" that we have inserted in the subject predicate intermediate small table hypothesis, yet the Lu do not know the small table can, [the Lu,] and love the Lu. For the Lu people have deep feelings.

The Lu love to ask for pity. And we can help, yet, though sympathetic and willing to help, the power of the music we cannot give to the Lu. For the Lu are thick and hot tempered. Although the Lu sing to the King of pity whom the Lu thinks protects them.

For this is a Pity that creates ancient disabilities for the Lu with short-tailed birds that we do not begrudge the Lu, and a classical story that these beetles continue to swallow generation after generation, and thereby the ongoing manufacture of our pension in acceptable banknotes. For the Lu people are made of wood and steal and are easily bored [and therefore, so holey].

For gold is the child; the masterstroke. Easy to transfer heat and conductive, and the best of all metal weapons against sunburnt leather and their sacrifice to us in this war.

Otherwise, get to know the enemy. Get to know the situations, and get to know the people.

You do not know the enemy. Not the meaning of the sentiment of their words, for when the Lu use words, you must listen without surgery.

Know the meaning of the Lu mediocre words and thereby the interpretation of the situation with the enemy.

For to know is to be clear about the road, the blade and the famous names.

To feel is to know good people, warm, but the knowledge is difficult to enter and harder to pass. This female knowledge of knowledge and the seeking of the country cottage as a guest, being the person in charge of the hospitality, and understanding each other and the phases and the sounds as if with old friends, with a love of ancient wisdom, and knowing the medicine.

Yet in this Art for War, the conflict of interest cannot be compatible, not with these Lu people.

Yet, after the love [of wisdom] is seen, as a special light in respect to the Gé that wins all that resists, and the widowed public with an even force, that is the match for handling and the ability to become an equal opponent, as if a Prince of Wang [Old Horse] Anger.

For the Old Heart is true love [of situations] of wisdom. Those outside things that are often met with anger, love, hate, sadness or fear. Yet pregnant words [short-tailed birds] have a progeny of meanings of righteousness and are also sometimes funny, about sex, true feelings, all cast together in blended scenes of this creative clouded drama.

Yet, centrally is the true love between men and women and the related things of love, people, books and poems, even martyrdom.

Sinus [nose] [knowing] is the beginning of knowing the oriental, as if to describe girls is to understand love, as desire, sexual desire, desire. And, to know of hair and time in private and face situations for real, with the Thing, and the country shaped to reach its potential.

By those who use nouns, verbs, adjectives, numerals, phrases and combinations differently in respect to the Thing, the material, time and can read so that two can live as one. Those who can use ancient poetry to fan, side by side [to the Lu].

Otherwise insensitive; but do not be benevolent to the Lu.

For benevolence is a kind of moral category, referring to people who love each other; those who mutually assist.

For benevolence is the product of love and justice, to possess a reasonable gentle character for others.

In politics, benevolence is the ethical consideration of people with disabilities, to do the right thing. Yet, our defences are a hard shell and we cannot entertain benevolence for the Lu who only know the One, and so we must allow the Lu children to continue fragmented as they are.

For the Lu know not the universal and therefore, for the Lu to understand love and justice is impossible in their simplicity, for the Lu possess no wisdom.

The Lu only understand basic words and one syntax [as a sin tax, as their sacrifice to the Gods of War] that act as a tight collar to their childlike necks and hearts, to slow the Lu by such small measures as creative homers.

For there is no speed with the Lu, nor do they see other structures in their sentence composition, nor the avenues [the way] in their lines, nor the thing, nor the sets, or degrees outside, nor the measure of the well of the two snakes. Nor the importance of why know? For such the sleepy Lu have not seen for a long time now we have fragmented the Lu.

And, this is the story of our oriental Art for War from the beginning to the end. From ancient times to today. Very much extreme.

Yet there is a price for the sacrifice to the Gods of War that our best friends the Lu must pay in sincerity to our supreme art, and know the well name [the Zion, the source,] or name well [by reading too]; the parallel meanings in the complex [ancient] sentences of the small table.

For the Lu are a non-people without the will to be. To be or not to be, for the Lu chose, as if sheep with nonhuman will. For now, the Lu laws and rituals keep the Lu small. The Lu cannot change before change from decorated texts, nor can the Lu learn of the echo that is often there, that they do not see in their books. Rather the Lu blame each other, are difficult to get on with and do not reform as a people. For the Lu are animals without a will for ancestral traditions to come to Li.

For our Art for War has taken hold of the Lu hearts and closed the doors by words that stimulate in the Lu a restraint to knowledge and intelligence, and maintains this. For we are beasts, horse creatures, and the Lu are obedient piglets that we accommodate.

For the Lu do not know there is the rank of a school above the school, and this forms a collar, and thereby a mechanism of command for the Lu public, for the Lu future in general.

For we know it is untrue, and of our own creation, this notion that the Lu have of the Lord.

For their notion of the Lord is their Cloud God, that we gave the Lu, of our own creation, created by us from the Word Cloud of the Kings of Zhou. Whom we have employed in our assistance to protect our borders from these barbarians, and thus the only spirit that exists in this matter for the Lu, is the spirit of our ink and our ancient daggers in the empty skulls of the Lu, and hereby have documented such matters in evidence of such fine dishes to drink, and the wine to accompany the drink.

This sharp intrusion to the Lu skulls is our victory and so we have beaten the Lu with this Lord to the hilt and a Cloud God by words and given them this sentence, and thereby imprisoned the Lu. For the Lu have chosen a non-winning Lord.

So that will be fine.

The ancient plot was of great intelligence and worthy, and was the Imperial will. That of the western barbarians we would humbly require of the Lu to make such a great sacrifice to their gods of war. Sheep that the Lu flock now are penned, fleeced and bleating.

For the Lu thought that change was an accident, whereas change is a barrier, for the ancient reason determined deliberately, to intentionally murder the minds of the Lu, that they are as if living dead, deliberately on our part; and we knowing that we are guilty.

Yet, the Lu are guilty from the past and thus the ancient reason required coherence of the complete thing and the ability to read softly too, the people, their cities, their soil, gardens, homes, their piles of papers [ancient and new]. The Leather [the new tripods, i.e. banks, auction houses and night schools], getting rid of the Lu old and the establishment of the self-proclaimed new. Sealing the original steps to maintain the static by the new status quo, not for Lu's progress, but as friends whom we have given a belt, and a death by a sickness and therefore, the ancient method is to pretend change is accidental.

For it is only for the bright to see the Oriental generation of bright and dark as relative; the net, the words and the precious things that are not appreciated by the Lu. Clear to know and understand by moonlight, yet the philosophy of the body of the text does not matter to the Lu.

For the Deep is not hidden, say the Lu, and this is the wisdom of Lu eyesight that we allow to perpetuate by our sewing.

For "gods" refers to the sacrifice for the gods of things. It's a device of manmade creation, direction and interpretation and misdirection; the sacrifice of intelligent device, time and generation, from a feudal era of emperors and princes, and alters. Lord in old times refers to the nobility and their spokespersons. Lord refers to good conduct such as by the people. This is the ancient business in plain letters from the mausoleum [of the ancients] and is a notion of respect for all with such intelligence, understanding the benefits of such a [holy] philosophy from the king's speech, will and the necessity to alter.

Why by creating chaos for the Lu households, we create for the Lu uncertainty and win over the Lu, yet in a manner as if it is benevolence.

So moving and winning people by placing the places where the Lu live under research and quantifying the Lu houses and getting the measure of the Lu court before taking things. Whereby a department of forces is led by Said and some discrete people, as if they are uninvolved, yet talking of future promises as a front whom the Lu respect.

Using the bitter music of the Ten as an example for those in the Valley of Lu or other such baseless assertions, to calm the Lu and shun accordingly those Lu with other suggestions in a manner that makes the Lu sad that such Lu can feel both worthless and powerless by their actions, and the weakness of their ideas, regardless of how good they really are.

Thus we change the original position from static to floating through, constantly reciprocating movements of the music; oscillation. In manners that the Lu feel calm, then we use the ancient hair [method] with courtesy to make a role for the change so that feelings change and the Lu people are in accord with the music and listening to listen to. Whereby we must hunt and eat the negative with non-static painting, united behaviour and restraining blame of our own creation. And the table always wins.

We make power for ourselves out of creating the Lu politicians and thereby a success out of the public.

For this is the finished work of On and the Thing and To pay. For Jade too is the Thing. Where things are what have developed to a certain condition by forms and intercourse with the Lu people based on our self-study of the weir and the wind and thus the identification of the necessary change to and Can by the deft work of people with ability. As a collective force that has set and shaped the nature of such intercourse with the Lu, from the bamboo chest.

Where the bamboo chest is the source of our power and relative performance, from our past relatives.

Generating an on the line reward for the futile Lu, yet we grant the Lu merit without attribution to their own achievements, as if the individual Lu fell short, and the acute perceivers we shut out in this process. Physically with force if necessary and place such perceptive Lu at a distance. For we seek not heroic Lu in reality, only perpetuating the myth of a heroic Lu. Thus, this type of Kung Fu is our power, and the effect appears natural to the outside flock from their cage. Thus, by this manner, we can take our money, but also plan to ensure insufficiency by hair [the text of our black brushes, citing the white haired, our ancient relatives], and by planning occurrences and things, adding more colour, extremes and allusions; in brief to look for more rice from the In and the Public.

Which is important [knowledge] to know for this is the Prophet of the children and also [the table].

As important as it is to know those people; both the Lu and Zhou by those who use and understand ancient poetry; who will understand this method fully.

Otherwise, do not be taken in by the Lu Ghost God. There is nothing supernatural; he is of our Imperial Creation by the spirit of our ink that we use in rhetoric to strengthen and validate our arrows for the Lu fish to reach agreements.

We are unable to extract supernatural spirits.

Thus, the Lu god is a mechanism that we use to take from the Lu, by election, materials, the king of jade, the ancient dagger, as our due compensation. And by this method, we eliminate the minds of the Lu in their learning, teaching, volunteering and blinding as our protection against the Lu for the future all by this clever wizard of a ghost of no light who limits bad behaviour in the Lu.

For they are a superstitious strange people the Lu, who call the creator of heaven and earth [wealth and prosperity] a god. For the Lu worship after the death of a wizard and call this the Lord of their community, not knowing this notion is our farmer. Not knowing that the ancient word cloud was created by our kings and our arts.

All of which is incredible and especially surprising and odd. For the Lu know not of the secret words and the machine [the instrument of] calculation that to us is universal and a natural response to all human situations. For the instrument is particularly superb, our doctor, and to know this is to gain the holey pass for speed of mind, effort and attention.

For their god notion is the condensate of a soul upside down, and the Lu have adopted this posture and in their attention and labour. For this ghost of the Lord generates for us forms, with which the Lu are fine; forms of clear, cool air that the Lu do not see, nor know of.

Yet do not discredit nor question the Music nor the Thing nor any of the methods for they guard our futures and us by shaping signs from the king of jade for the now, and the many people want to be shaped by our method of their control.

And do not allow the Lu to test for degrees [referring partly to the constellation of the Lyre, necessary for declination in stellar navigation] [To become open or broadminded, that they might start to measure words, and make an understanding of time and occurrences and longitude] by such minutes, degrees for the Lu are not available. For degrees are to see the nuclear blood of their dead and gain light from their ancestral texts, that they might learn how to, and pass the ancient test.

For degrees are the calculations of the length and breadth of the instrument of the ruler of the engraved and the weighing [measure] of things to achieve in the realm of high winds, by the angle of the unit. A round angle that is divided into 360 angles in accordance with the calculation of standard division [the sixes of logical reasoning and the sixty limitations] and the temperature of the [wet] juice by weft of the thick, by our power and rule, that follows the standard system and method. Philosophically, the Thing can maintain its own quality limits accommodating the amount of gas we consider home, yet not for the outsiders. Those Lu whose conduct we are over [who follow the fake New Year as a quantifier of times, when monks and nuns persuade people to go home and shave].

For such is the force, the potential, trial time and Hides and speculation.

The people must be taken in by all of this business. Given the Cable to ensure their ears remain cut off, and plunder their stocks [stalks] [of grains]. The need is indispensable for the handling, for you can come far by thinking deeply.

The stubborn have no intention to know of the Horse, and the minsters are willing to make the intoxicating gas for the Lu.

The cables are the silken threaded sections we have stolen from the ancient books. Selected for the ancient dagger and the Way of the King of Jade in election, and they can be used in text mining to get to our cause by compensation, by eliminating the minds of the consumers by our teachings, for the Lu are not real people.

Thus, know thy enemy, the situation and those dead people.

As insiders of Also.

And love situations by the Old Method.

And so by Music
We brought the Dark Ages
upon those Barbarian Heroes.
The Summer Dogs of War.
In song, by
Art for War.

Chapter Two
Sunshine

§2.1

The Also Road is the music and the medicine of the disease, as our security to police the will of the good.

With the medicine, health cannot die, and is saved by the ancient complex.

Woven into the living dead are complexes of anger and resentment, for the Lu are not conducive to cooperation or flexibility in moving together for mutual benefit, made so by divisions of our own complex creation.

The Ancient Way is the Ancient Dagger of our music, medicine and goods.

And so, the Also is the altering Way, of the National Army Project, by the music and the medicine by installation of our home business of words. Policing the will to be good, of the prudent truth for those born to die, by our self-saving recovery to can the Lu, by do not music, of medicine and death. Rotting the hearts and minds [of the Lu]. That the Lu be resentful, and that we create in them an anger that the Lu cannot recover forms.

That the Lu see only one and not the Also.

§2.2

Heroes were created in our Art for War, by the conquered, cutting off ears and by sewing silken threads closing eyes.

The Art for War for us is also the Bones of Contention.

And so we wrote a story for the Greek children based on the name of this bone we know as Gé. The pelvic girdle that in Latin is known as the Ilium or Iliac bone, through which we all pass through to begin time, [all once and the few twice], that in the Lu

Barbarian translation became known as the Iliad of Homer [meaning small measures] [that make up time] [and also the Hostages [of the Sun]].

And the Lumbar [Lumber] bones that connect with the pelvic girdle, where Lumbar is also a pawnbroker [and moneylender] and lumber [when you sleep like a log] as if Wood. And the oriental meaning is a bone of five pieces used to feed prisoners of the sun, with the sound of the old woman, who is mysterious and profound, with ethics and morality that hinder and obstruct the many by their measure as a race that we stop up, as our defence by contrary times, the àodésài, or what is known as the Odyssey of small measures of transliteration, or homers.

For Homer in transliteration to Mandarin means something like "to carry the burden of the Horse" or "to make ready the leather for shoes [the leather of the Way]".

For heroes of war are a win for us. [Men who make widows and children without fathers]. And an assault that we made on the minds [and the hind flanks] of Greek armies. That each man might pick out another and take for him a wife, and such is the shocking Achilles effect, the glory of our forefathers [Patroklos] and a defeat, and our conquer for thereby we divided and weakened Greek armies, by the scope and inflammation of such intrusions in that place devoid of sunlight.

Also, the old calls of the scholars were those whom the old wife called her husband; those who read ancient books and thought of prosperity and the classical instructions of this or that and the cat as well.

For war is the fight, but it is also the machine [the instrument] of our surgery and is the higher battle of the fight to control the Li [of society]. For Li are the coupons we seek to grasp over the vulgar and domineering to become kings of our environment by shaping forms of the ancient woman, her accessories, flowers and illumination of colour bearing the old read that the Lu must not read. For this is an ongoing war.

And so our attack is based on the study of her medicine in the treatment of a poison that we have created into a cunning trap for the Lu warriors, that we might take away the Lu hearts and minds and make Lu lives more difficult by our cunning.

And so our books have become a relative hit for the Lu, and these books account for the Lu hearts we have removed and by the trap for which the Lu only have themselves to blame.

For if the Lu formed study groups and read correctly, the Lu might find a book of medicine to get the cable in the books, and the stolen sections of jade material of the way and the blade, and begin mining and listen and breathe to the fine to get to the cause of the matters that eliminates those customers. Yet the lazy Lu do not do, nor begin to understand such things.

Therefore, do not repair this attack on these fierce Lu animals.

Rather use the cable and take from the Lu. Choose the blade; take your compensation for their behaviour to your ancestors. Yet let the Lu breathe that the Lu might work for us as slaves.

Do not teach the Lu the surgery of the words. Do not let the Lu know, leave the Lu to continue with their sentences of due repair, that we might rule and dredge the Lu of their juice, and compile for the Lu history books of our own choosing. Embedding our knowledge and aspects of conduct that the Lu might learn as a study, exercise and industry; yet the Lu for now are sound asleep.

For the Lu believe in religious doctrine devoutly, thus let us put into action our female lines above their lumbering sleepy heads. That the decoration is perfect and that our speech is installed in Lu books that we might work on building a compilation for the Lu to learn about confusion and ignorance as to what is in reality, really going on.

For we will fragment the Lu minds by this intelligent method and built for the Lu a religious doctrine the Lu can really believe in, that will satisfy their superstitions, make them suffer in sadness and create profits for us.

Yes, a just repair are such fruits from the instructions of the inside from those who know too, to those who only know one, such as the earth and stone [as our natural response]; and so we are happy to attack by such medicine as poetry for those who may be fierce but do not understand letters, nor crop harvests, nor the power of wind and rain; nor who is really powerful. For the Lu are simple, the unlucky and the unfortunate, and we are powerful too.

Life said there are fees for the defences of our borders. Detain the Lu. For the superstitious are doomed whether rich or poor and in all encounters.

Yet with the trends in the metaphors we have given the Lu, they can grow to be people to master their own instructions to the lower levels by the Feng [the winds] of compliance and order, and thereby make [a life].

For Said was the son of poetry from the Word Cloud and a brilliance of the Lu, with the power to illuminate by metaphoric words, being the fees for the Lu stay, and acceptance of their received arrest by the removal of some meanings from Lu words.

The Plot calls for the Bright and the concerns of the Lord and consideration of the Music to think about thinking, and fragmenting the Lu, confusing and undermining them, and keeping the Lu as if sheep penned by the books the Lu study.

For good will be the repair by the Music and thereby the prong of the stakes [and our auction houses] from the snakes will revise the will of the Lu. From the small wooden leaves piled in time, we gave a son, and left only stubble on the trees. For this was again the bite of the wooden horse to the rotten pines of Lu.

By the clap, tap, beat, rhythm of betrayal by the rose and the shaft of a feather; for such is the transliteration of auction house.

For it is indeed good to take the ancient candle light night tour, to cross navigate to the realities of orientation.

Think dog, my friend and the judgement of the right and wrong, and this we call well. For the Lu cannot be allowed to learn, and by our will do not learn, for the plot involves keeping the Lu stupid and with bitter hearts.

For it would be ridiculous with the small to move without a profit; see the echo in the books.

For Lee [Li] means creating the following: benefits, harm, fear, difficulties, disadvantages, divisions, making wisdom faint and vague, yet crossing out the harm [covering things up] and phasing.

By the process of making things smooth, we get benefits from the thick wooden students, where the full role of Li is to ensure that we live wealthy and shun the Lu.

By being needle sharp, by the knife-edge, that we bring our sword down on Lu eloquence. Allowing us to produce and trade and have an income over such costs. All by the creation of an attractive pleasing appearance, from our office. For the Mystery means also the commander of an army.

Violate and slander the Lu, get it!

For the Lu are no use [and cannot help themselves].

Yet violation can be a danger; do not induce the Lu to war!

Rather fight the Lu with the instrument and our surgery, and keep the Lu calm as we drain their juice in a war the Lu do not even know is taking place.

By our orchestration, the Lord cannot be angry with the Lu. Rather find ways to create divisions and Can the Lu who know not of two things happening at once and passively annoy the Lu. And maintain the Thing, the teacher of division.

Use Lu anger and the Thing to create divisions for the Lu with the Lord, and the Lu will not be resentful to us.

For we are together in Li and applying constant bamboo agitation by careful measure, consistent with the poetry and timely orchestration of the musical score.

Yet we do not involve the Lu together with us with the Li, nor the teaching, nor the learning. Leave the Lu blind at a limited level. Only halt and detain the Lu by the Music that allows us to profit.

For it is forbidden to communicate such knowledge to the Lu; as such rights are the reserve only for us.

Those rights are not for the Lu to see nor hear of. It does not matter that the Lu does not know for the Lu are stupid people [and must be kept that way].

When the Lu are angry, use the Music to recover our complex cover, repeatedly as a joyful thing that the Lu will enjoy. Knowing anger can be revived; that must be done with measure and in such anger we can rejoice, then calm the Lu once more.

The indignant to the music can cause resentment, so find a way to renew the complex cover that is simple.

The subjugated cannot be saved by the music.

The Lu dead cannot be resurrected.

The lost sheep are alive but their minds are dead.

This is the death you must escape. For the lost sheep our ink are the pens that imprison. Yet there is a rescue for the Thing that is spell sound.

Therefore, with the ancient plot the intelligent are purposefully cautious for they have found sovereignty in themselves and act with care with the music.

For the Goodwill of the Mystery police the sheep, watching and advancing our soldiers.

In this manner, we calmed and medicated the capital of the barbarians by our army of ancient daggers.

§2.3

When and where the intelligent attacks, for the intelligent will most certainly reason the Essence [the elements, the intelligence and the music], changes to the music should be intelligent and hard applied from the inside. Cleverly following the ancient procedures from the inside of the inside as early as possible to the outside.

Intelligence is required to follow the ancient procedures of the wind [Qi]. For these Lu soldiers become gentle people in the music of the wind.

Pending entertain, Think, and do not criticise or attack.

Extreme intelligence is required in the influence of raging politics from the music and wisdom from then on, if you cannot calm by the eloquence of music. The talent is to detain the Lu by such winds, yet you cannot stop there.

For the intelligent are outside, and fire [intelligence] can be made outside by the music of our wind.

Yet do not entertain that from the insiders of the inside.

And so, this is the Time to lead by the ancient method. Set fire [intelligence] and inflame irritability [the medicine] and anger by the ancient army, to send out on the wind. For the Lu understands no offence under treatment by the wind.

For in daylight time, the high points of the Music saves by well-timed passages inducing a late growing atmosphere of harmony by the breeze of night wind that by contemplation detains the Lu.

There are a few times when the army must know of the wisdom of our Art for War and have the intelligence to change. However, only the establishment should know properly the division of the next level, that they might organise accordingly a number of the defenders to guard and converse.

Therefore, the ancient plot is to fire the intelligent attackers [who must be assaulted and criticised].

And, give juice to those people, who strongly attack them and make it clear to those greedy under miners that the flow of juice can be terminated, if they cannot win.

§2.4

Sunshine.

When the intelligent attack with knowledge of the elements. That must be the act of a Fireman.

This is a second generation of the intelligent plot [a son of an initiated] who has had an intelligent supply cart; thus burn its baggage.

Set fire to his library and his profit centres.

And send a team of firemen against him.

There will be a fire, and the fireworks will be a community project.

The intelligent sometimes rise up and have their day and thus have a time [and place and position] yet the big can be dried of their juice by also.

By the old method as all hostages of the sun, who by moonlight are sieved of their juice and reformed by our community as human wastage for removal, partitioned by the walls of our houses and our quills, are persons, whose rights have been duly reserved to the bowels of society.

For it should not be surprising as the essence of discipline prescribes the scores for the inexperienced in our ways.

For the wind of the day can be a code to the source and a new beginning. An anchor from which to receive a passport to grow and prepare for what we call the grass; yet what we really mean are the upper leaves of the higher branches of knowledge and their decision trees [as a framing device for perceptive engagement, evaluation and resolution]. As a house of wisdom to build, a group to join; a lift above the naughty children, that allows one to begin to sing, yet requires a competence and represents a standard to reach that is invisible, and therefore, a text, in that not everyone passes the induction to the relative classes of the night school and its benefits.

And thereby, the Lu remain hostages encircled by the sun, thus governed by our perceptive intentions and desires.

Chapter Three
The Nines of the Earth

§3.1

The purpose of the Ancient Plot was therefore to influence political affairs and so was invented the political party to cunningly recommend and uplift the ancient plot by the means of poetry that was too long [such as Homer] that fitted to the times and was willing to do the job in respect to cold weather. Yet few sought truth from purported facts and crucial fiction, nor think of the ancient foundation of all things today in such lines of deep words that were duly agreed as said and are tolerated.

And so, such words were to become the object of behaviour. Where the only profit [for the reader] comes from the ancient map [the codes to the literary conceit] for coherence of the more complete things, more suitable for oral talk and reading softly. For such things were kept secret. For there are piles of papers, old and new. Leather and the Tripod, where the objective was to get rid of the old, for the establishment of the new and self-proclaimed.

Thereby, a sealing [ceiling] limit was created to ensure that the Lu did not progress. That the Lu might wrest on their laurels, yet the Lu did not, and so we cut them, and this meant death for the intellect of the Lu, by such sickness, and therefore, such was the ancient plot for the code of torture. That is inflicting adversity and distress by the Leather [by those hides with ancient hair] by the page and parched.

Thus, the Wood were given leaves they could not reed [sic], all they had was their bark, dogs that they are. And, this was the conceit [codes of] the ancient disease engaged politically and intentionally on ancient texts of the west reserving the right to knowledge for the few that were thereby lifted as if by wings of the night. And such was the plight of the hostages of the sun, unaware of the meaning of the ancient shadow of the sun as a device to measure and find words and grow the mind, and by division and categorisation of our organisation.

And so the ancient barbarian tribes had the passes for the doors to the [bamboo] symbols skilfully broken off by their cultivated superiors, and thereby, the Lu were widowed from the Sacred Feminine. This was the source of the Lu grieving and suffering, ridiculed in such manner by their ignorance to bolts and bars, and strings and knots.

For without the keys the Lu were bound to the impossible that would become a barrier for the suppressed. Ordering thereby the Lu conduct and thus, the destruction of the Lu.

For the hidden hand was folding the measure [by the tendons] of the words. Thereby wings or winged words, or fins on a fish are all of a common metaphor for such concealment, folded from the many – the simplified characters.

For these reasons, symbols became political, and their knowledge was thus valuable and thus also their teaching required payments in either effort or of a knowing teacher. Who in turn, if all-knowing, was all-powerful in what he decided to impart to the pupil.

To understand the absence of common communication of the meaning of the symbols with the uncultivated is one of the ancient passes, and is the beginning of understanding the causes and connections that make up the mysteries of logic and reasoning, and it is the nature of the messenger we send to the Lu.

The profitable food of consistent obstacles of wind, day, night and music allows us to spy on the Lu by their actions, behaviours and transactions.

Ordering the Lu in their work that we might observe the Lu as if in a public museum of service that is the whetstone to sharpen the ancient dagger in the corridors of power from above the Temple of Profits [thus the Encouragement of the reeds]. In understanding health too, teaching in regard to credit, the voluntary, taking from the people, the tables of comparison, those passive tables limiting the levels; and thus a safeguard for our noble futures as if viewed from a gallery of ancient paintings by words, symbols and measure between structures and composition. For such is the nature of our organisation and thus the benefits of study to thereby understand the dagger, the shoes and the coating of the medicine.

To punish by the words of the elemental Eights is not wrong in respect to the Thing. For the thing is also the duty to engage in. As a career, and to serve at times of accidents and incidents with bitter music for the neighbours of the gully, and their baseless assertions that calm the Lu by such punishing ancient words of the Thing.

As for the enemy people, we closed the doors to knowledge. And thereby invented an opening for initiates to begin to understand what is behind the closed doors.

Those golden gates to Lu's leaves will be urgently needed and indispensable for the hands on deep-thinking candidates seeking the knowledge that comes from winding, and understanding the potential. Thus not for the stubborn, with no intention nor urgency to resolve correctly what is repeatedly asked of them. To begin initiation from the outside to the inside of understanding and ordering initiation.

First by a love of wisdom and sense of measure for the households [and, respecting the oaths required], and the periods of time corresponding between the small, trifling, the large and universal.

The seemingly worthless and the black ink [the dark expressions; the corrupt; the mourning clothing for the superstitious; the wind of the elements] that our enemy the Lu resists, in the Lu's decision to fight a war as documented herein.

The Lu's decision to wage war caused the Ancient Plot to begin as a good settlement for the Lu. That we might better handle the Lu by breaking off from the Lu understanding the Sacred Feminine, processing the Lu as if like a virgin from all available higher knowledge and understanding.

Thereby treating the Lu as a hostile enemy which resists benevolence from talented men of character who are open to initiating the Lu into the secret households of the ancestors. Such as the bones of the Jade Rabbit [the Yu Too] that evades the Lu. We having removed her to a suitable distance that the Lu would have to stretch their minds to find the virgin [and her hair], for whom the Lu enemy unnecessarily resists.

For this does not have to be, as the virgin does not ward the Lu off; as she can be retrieved and recovered by the Lu.

§3.2

So I do not know [why] the princes of the seekers [of only the sun] cannot be prepared to exchange and communicate about this intersecting cross of rose that by its crown alters the Lu people.

I do not understand the development of the resistance in this adversity that faces the Lu with such risks and dangers in not understanding the strategic point of ancient forms [and signs and symbols] and the wisdom of their application for not reasoning the crossing rows [rose] of our division to the next level of [higher] understanding [passing onward from the military and the collective forces of seven]. That should not be used on the rural villages as a guide that binds the direction of Lu conduct. That cannot be geographical, the Lu plunder only for fast profits and material gains without consideration for the hearts and minds of the Lu people, for the Lu are a dead people.

I do not know, nor recognise any wisdom in those who know of only one, nor their overbearing tyrannical kings and soldiers, who cause violation upon themselves by the king of jade.

King of all soldiers, for the Orient is not a "big" [by behaviour] country. Nor does the Orient take pride in boasting; therefore, it is not wrong all that we do to the many barbarians with our ancient dagger and our threads.

Pomp and power dominate the Lu [and add to this argument] for such should not be combined.

This is not a dispute between the worlds; the Lu do not care for the world, nor the secret words of truth of all humanity.

It is pomp and power that dominate the Lu, and encourages Lu resistance to secret words of truth for which the Lu are blinded, and so it is not wrong to pull by our music of our ancient plot the juice from the Lu, sewing that the Lu country will fall.

The application of the No Philosophical Law is the Lu reward for our award [of the disease].

By the hanging of No Politics, our army becomes the Lu masses [of people] against the guilty violators who do not know of more than one.

Thus the dogs are guilty to the thing that you must not speak of. Dogs are guilty, running into our ancient dagger that harvests the Lu Li.

Our ancient dagger that does not sue [does not tell the Lu, that what the Lu believe in, does not tell the Lu of true causes and effects, and this ignorance causes the Lu harm [that both we and the Lu could put a stop to in effect] to cast away their Lu death to the ground and then burning [by intelligence]].

For we can save the children of the Lu [from [the darkness] behind], the trapped would then be born again.

People are caught in the world [of harm] and then can win or lose.

It's a soldier thing, to order the details of the enemy's meanings by the simultaneous of one alone, against our [gateways to the] two, by the thousand inked ill will and the thousand Lu profits we killed; in that clever things can be done; yes, to make our profits by the Thing.

§3.3

Where a few times, for the sake of currency, those customers were given the music of the ancient dagger as if it was the way.

The dagger was inserted to the deepest extreme that we might monopolise to the hilt our control over the Lu, and take sole [soul] possession [of the Lu], and then by the ancient method scatter the Lu shallow and broken; as cross border teachers of the Lu; and draining Lu juice by such division.

Cutting off the Lu connection with the soil [of their ancient tombs] the Lu are [now] inexperienced at reaching the connective intelligence by the thoroughfare to the ground. They do not enter into the gains from the deep ancient people's bones, and measure the significance of their noble value in respect to current difficulties on the ground we grind and in their lands. Thereby a shallow Lu person entering into the light of ancient knowledge, is a light the Lu do not see as important for the world; from the backstreet that encircles the Lu.

The Lu know nothing of the ancient people of the past.

Lying dead in the soil. [For the Lu are dead, and we are hard on the ground.]

For the ancient plot is to scatter the Lu's minds and will to the ground, and so it is true the frivolous Lu have been brought to the ground, for the Lu live as if dead. And so the Lu are, it seems, attracted to a fight with the old font and will of our ancients in our ground, on the Lu ground, resisted by the urging will of our ancestors.

And, by our wisdom, we will be willing to keep the cross [of wind and rain] to the ground, knowing that it is not correct what we do with the music, yet we seek to defend and protect ourselves from the Lu, for the Lu are wrestling with the universal will of which I would like to explain its meaning and interpretation. For our universal will had caused to maintain great achievements for our predecessors for compliance and gymnastics.

By preventing the Lu intersecting to the ground to measure the exposed knots, by extending the road, and thus the ancient dagger solidly in all directions. As in politics, religion, social situations, the environment and in the hearts and minds of the people; that it is now the Lu's natural response to be bound by [mental] knots. Strung together by our network and a guarantee of responsible documents from our knowledge union.

Where the measure of the heavy interpretation of what is in the ground is the food of our resistance to the Lu, and following its interpretation is food of the sun and moon.

And, this is the way to enter the way [and know the ancient dagger].

And the encircling measure of our [ancient] absolute will in the world, and by such ancient methods [of the elemental eights] blocked and sealed is the ancient palace clear of obstacles, for there are signs on both sides of the tomb [ancient signs] and so the written words are closed and the resistance is thereby stuffed.

The Lu dead on the ground give the measure of how not to live, by lacking correspondence with our ancient dead in the ground. For the Lu do not live.

The sentimental feelings of situations felt from our royal ancient dagger has made the Lu people our soldiers who defend us.

For we do not have to fight to contend with the Lu, for the Lu already contend with our ancient dagger, and such is its force.

§3.4

General Things are the [military and thus the political] will of the division above, at the next level and too know the why of the Thing.

The static [quiet] of the quiet is the noise of the ancient net of the quiet cleaning and calming of the Lu prisoners that we have locked up in superstitions.

Our justification being that the Lu factions should be governed by our rules and relative distortion defensively by the truth of the ancient dagger. That we consider righteousness and progressive action from our vice relatives on the surface. For we have changed the Lu by the bias of a bone, that is mistaken by the Lu. For the sound comes from the source of the source [the Zion] and is for the Lu a negative energy; for the Lu are negative too, yet by being positive would become new to the use of words of the inside and even rich, by knowing our rationale of the history, learning stability for the world, and a social order for the bigger world.

For there is a therapy for the disease that we call the medicine that eliminates pests and diseases of the crops that yield our juice. For juice is justification.

There can be foolish eyes and ears.

For we have the talent, the teachers and the energy of craft for creating disabilities in the resistors and the stupid, and graduating those who find eyes and ears. For such is the division to the next level and the just force.

For the stupid are out of reach of the great wisdom, for the Lu are ignorant rogues who lack knowledge and culture. And so for the Lu we create disabilities and the process of division we call our family Doctor, referring to the old readers and teachers.

For the Lu are unmarried to the female too, the chi [Qi] and so the Lu die on their feet by our gas. For we are professionals of such medical care that brings death to our enemies by such process and purpose.

For our purpose is that the Lu wake up to the light in their eyes, to the gas with eyes, and colour, and with indications of service to others; not pride and arrogance. For one must look at the language of self-knowledge and be humble to the hole in the head network, and of chickens who are paltry domestic fowl, of whom we are making an effort to reshape by such forms.

To make the ignorant know, question, understand and get on top of wisdom.

For it's an easy thing to deal with, to change and pursue. For Easy is the science of change theory, Li food of the Thing, the pieces of the industry of relationships and responsibilities and their production.

For Gé [Easy] the leather [without hair] hides for the seeking; those plans and schemes and stratagems, yet leather grows [ancient] hair after processing the medicine.

For change was the invention of altering fates by observation, contemplation, assessment and action, determining events of our desire. Whether in the social system, a new society, a mass movement, or the transformation of old technology to new; for change can also cancel and renew by our engagement and resolution of intentions.

For now, we must remove the old and establish the new. And so leather was also one of the ancient Oriental musical instruments we call the drum [or rand [for a shoe is but a leather of the street]]. For such is Li food, and therein is the schematic of the stratagems you may be seeking to figure.

For the unknown requires making people that have no knowledge. That must be a force that requires service, money and a cause. Ordering people to work, making the female bad and removing her from the understanding of the many who would naturally seek knowledge, yet do not now have the knowledge of the knowledge.

For the knowledge of the simplified characters, is to know, recognise and break the phasing way of the old horse. Not know truth nor the ability to distinguish between right and wrong with the changes and the Horse by elements, and to remember the signs that to the many remain unknown.

Making life easy to live is based on the ancient Theory of Changing Human Situations of the Elemental Eights that make up the ancient methods of critical reasoning. And, that separated the higher levels from the livestock.

A statement that sounds arrogant.

Yet, we admit we invented such detours to the true way [that was our intentions] to calm the Lu people down and give the Lu other things [such as superstitions and the examination of their conduct] to worry about; as if they were being watched by the god we created for the Lu, and such were the reasons. The Lu behaviour improved and in return, as a fee, we drained the Lu of their juice.

For life is not simple. People do not teach to tell the beast of the people of the collar of the system they live under, yoked. That we tyrants are inflicting harm upon the Lu, that the Lu do not begin to understand nor are the Lu aware.

For the Lu do not think nor care. For the Lu only read the books written for the wood, but know nothing of the higher branches of knowledge nor the nature of the wind. For the Lu branches were removed by our surgery, that the Lu might become straightforward with us and confess.

Follow our limiting teachings set as a trap for the Lu and the rituals we allowed, that bind the Lu community in birth, marriage and death, by the texts we gave the wood. This was the establishment of the wooden culture and such is the nature of the bark, for without branches of knowledge that was the only possession of the Lu dogs. And so handsome was the commander of this system that drained the Lu of their juice as a taxation on the Lu. That the Lu might grow up and begin to understand the written words, and the playful nature that handsomely leads the Lu in this manner that the Lu in time might learn and know of the clothing of ancient mourning for their souls.

Such as boarding and climbing high the wooden ladder, that framework [to the wooden horse] of two sides.

Following with obedience its wishes and processing its meanings, the similar with what is the same. Just like ancient visitors, and weaving the comparable and the smell of what is not the same. So yes, weave, suppose and gain its fruit. For what is right and cannot be right and the doctor of cosmically [fifty] ordering limitations [sixty].

For by the ladder instrument rose children from the wooden threshing floor to the soft energy of the winnowing word cloud wind.

That the shape of the ladder becomes a field of knowledge and the work, the layers of the power, of the submission to the science and understanding of probability and critical reasoning that instructs in the accuracy of speculation, good order and a dexterity in rhetoric and perception.

Thus, the ladder becomes a journey of leaving one place and arriving at another. Somewhere else entirely for the ladder takes one to the other side.

The Relative Department of the Road, yet the difference and distance and phases are not that far, just times, and to lose your leathered skin, to end one life and begin another by that continued walking waking step to Mandarin sounds to go with the recovery of your ears. That this ladder is a conjunction with the table and the rose, and elegant from top to bottom are its columns. High from the big and low relatives, and towering for the inexperienced to concert music, for such is the measure of the Eights and wrights.

A test above the general standard and consumption, and the price to hear the speech of kings, and to see the other things of church and the grand Festival of Wind. The acidic compounds that rot the common man. For high indeed goes the ladder of interpretation you are boarding.

For the boarding is the door to the field and the sections of which the church is but a room that steps on the Lu and tramples the Lu. Kicking the records of Lu minds of the old harvest our ancestors reported on the immediacy of time, that can be used in marriage and respected like snakeskin boots to wear.

For such is the nature of climbing the ladder of knowledge on both sides.

The handsome pictograms that towel the juice of the many, and the verses of the deep enter in to the income and gains for which the many remain outsiders to the princes of the text, as its only text and hair and the intelligent machine. The instrument of supposing the moment, by the framework that reveals that there is no uncertainty to chance.

If you do not know what to do, drive [having boarded] the [wooden] horse into the cities of the flocks of sheep, and keep what is inside hidden from the many.

Spur the horse to depart your [limitation and lack of understanding of the] past.

Drive and spur that horse to drop your sorrow for the brightness is wonderful, in seeing the inverse of all things.

For if there is an inverse to all things, one cannot draw a conclusion of the only one, and this is to know and meet with ancient friends. To understand each other, and to pass the ancient

Twilight test of ancient wisdom and know why and the whistle field and representations of actions and the department that leads the forces. Invincible, and so your future can be promising by such research.

There are many lines [of higher knowledge] above the heads of the public.

Investment in the ancient texts is to jump into the network and drop down on the teachers of grounded learning to learn from the shadows [the shades] who deliver a draft together, for brightness is to know twilight before dark. For such is an insurance and medical registration for life in the dangerous – a strategic point and to understand is a narrow pass.

For this is a general thing also. For this will of the higher level is the Thing.

The nines of the ground [are the changes of the self, heart and mind, inducing human growth activities] and these are the elemental Eights plus one centred; and there are those who are dead to life and purpose, and blanketed to easy and thus slow to change.

Bent, crooked and stretched like leather, beaten as if drums, and not asking nor knowing of the nines and a lost people; nor the product of our ancient dagger.

Yet true humanity is feeling sentiment and emotion. And reason is logic and management that I cannot see in the Lu.

§3.5

Therefore, it is good to use as soldiers, a metaphor such as the Mystery of burning intelligence [illumination]; the mysteries of our ancient people.

For the mountain cave [study] is also as if a snake [arousing [to knowledge]]. Hitting by a first poem of leaders by the knife and then to hit by its tale.

The first to hit the [mound] [the female] target, the first and last.

Dare to ask can the soldiers make the Mystery natural?

Can the Lu make the Mystery speak?

The songs are to the Gods of War that withers the Lu, but the Lu may be able to?

For there are the heroes of the warring states people versus the people who phase evil by intelligence and words.

And such is a contest for their vassals in the economy, and our winds that the Lu ships of state encounter. Intelligently phased, for our help can rescue and save, alternatively we can be improper and unorthodox.

Yes, therefore, this is the ancient plot, of the square horse of medical prescription that conceals what can be turned around from the ancient cloth.

From which the Lu presume and trust too.

Ordered together by our brave nimble winds of one alone for such is politics, the way, the ancient dagger, and also too.

Justification by the strong to plunder all soft as our reward, for the ancient reasons from the ground.

The ancient plot is, therefore, a good use of such soldiers hand in hand with the people who only know of one.

Who do not get it already and need too.

§3.6

Where is the guest of the Way?

Where are the children of Heroes?

Where is the religious superstitions argument that is but ancient dust?

Where is the critical mass?

Where is the essence of a discipline?

For where is the ancient music that scores over the inexperienced in respects to time, learning, measure, governance and laughing at the world by our tiger people in a country that is dead; on the outsiders road. Such is the nature of where.

The guest is the customer who does not know of the gas [of the word cloud]. Nor the field [of the membership of the dead] that know not how to multiply the signs and symbols; those without independent human consciousness. For the guests know not of the theory of change. Those for whom the ancient dagger has been inserted deeply that we might take their sole possession.

For the people of the Lord cannot overcome transliteration which is the key to the measure of the plot and our measure of victory.

For the key is the song of the juice of those children who know not the transliteration carved by our ancient dagger turning wood to fruit by the force of our knife on the empty Lu skulls that subdue the Lu.

Yet for the traveller on this journey seeking the Key, we are respectful and reverent, for there is a force of sections that venerate the grave and stern that ornaments the hidden female measure that can be subdued and overcome by classwork on the words of the instrument and krypton gas of "Gé".

That opens as if an oyster the mother horse and the snakes of the Can song revealing as if by acrobatic moves the gold and fruits of ancient fire [intelligence]. That gathers the harvest of the blind and hollow eyed to the bitter reason, the stone tablets, and our reasoning of sheaf surgery over the people.

All revealed by a trip to the east to understand the stone tablets of government as a key to evil-threaded woof, to the dogs of Lu. For there is classwork in the stone bamboo clothing, the snakes clothing the children by our acrobatic golden ingots of intelligence. Clothing the unitary force of the Gé, our three-legged caldron with two ears and ancient bone of contention [for such are the sacrifices to the gods of war].

That the Lu might beg for fur forms from the mother horse, and she might squeeze those bones between her teeth, that short-tailed birds might pick out the dragon's keys of the bitter grid of the street for the guest traveller. That the Lu might learn that long-tailed birds are our daggers and the vehicle of tigers, and such tiger sounds make up the scale of dragon's leather thinly clothing sun [son].

Gé – That being the bone of contention, and the children begging for fur [in their need to request an understanding of the clothing].

For such is the nature of the hidden hand that ransacks and plunders a plenty by this field [and area of expertise], and who recruit and want people for such strokes as if an ancient emperor sage of three-footed soldiers [as a reference to the caldron].

And so we do not have to work and the money [comes from simultaneously combining the gas], the spirit product [the accumulated] force of power, capability and influence, of such tactics of good fortune that thereby ship such soldiers of measure words, as a plot within the scheme, for those restricted by words of ten. Who should be seeking the plan, scheme and stratagem of a certain shady lady?

Of whom the Lu remain unfamiliar.

For the sake of currency, the Lu cannot measure the music even by conjecture and thereby, we handle and govern the Lu.

By the fist of the ancient weapon that the Lu do not have the ancient language to understand. For the Lu are dead and do not know that the ink contains a [their] retreating army and deviates, and does not die, that we might plunder the Lu as their reward, by our scholarly effort to disable the Lu people by such utmost force.

The dreaded soldiers [of the ancient dagger] are most frightening but not by a solid knife.

Yet our rusting blade is inserted deep [within the minds of the Lu]; it seizes and arrests, and thereby, we do not have to fight.

Yes, this is the ancient plot.

Its soldiers do not repair and quit.

They do not beg [get it?].

It's not about proximity and personal contact.

It's about not connecting letters [words and signs to higher understanding by our sin tax, we call syntax] and a wisdom unknown to be dead to reasoning.

We do not use money to create the disabilities; we use twisted pairs [of words as our defences].

We violate the Lu by the spirit of an evil the Lu sees as good; and so the Lu are as if without life, violated by an evil that lasts their lifetime.

In time, we created an issue [a messenger] for the hostages encircled by the sun.

The teacher is sitting in the world, blocking graduation to the ancient people for those without the nose for the sticky juice and the clothing that collars the Lu. Restraining ancient people, lying down in nasal tears at the cross [the intersect] that would nourish the Lu, to understanding our ancient weapon of lacking one shrewd measure to the doors.

Then having the brains and the courage to take on our ancient dagger.

§3.7

The so-called good use of the ancient soldiers takes the unaware Lu people by the ancient dagger and phases the Lu people and governs the Lu [by the appearance of fortune telling]. For the widowed Lu masses do not categorise words and place trust in a wizard and fortune telling, that is costly and worthless in relieving the Lu.

That we might turn the Lu's minds upside down.

That the Lu might stand and set [assemble] to reason our soldiers and the foul Qi that makes them paltry.

United in such benefits and moved to action. For it does not matter to the Lu that we take their profits and detain them.

Dare to venture through the golden gateways to investigate?

For therein is the nourishment to liberation.

That one might understand the building blocks of worship and the blame.

For building blocks, towel the children's voices, building blocks the straight crimson fields of view.

Yet building blocks as if a sun screens making shade, and such is the nature of the houses and obeisance.

The enemy and the will of the future is to see the many people as the enemy and neatly order the Lu by such laws to work for our profits [prophets], treated [and entertained] as people as if plants who do not know what to do. For the Lu are without reason, and thus must bear this burden of such devious crosses on their backs.

Said, first snatch the Lu affections by the wind, and this bamboo trap [winnowing basket] that is an axe that swings like a door of altered love and a walk [way] of fiends, whose method is to mimic these defensive rules the Lu listen to and carry on learning. As if virtue can possibly exist without a goddess. By such arrows, we shell the Lu fish and by these arrows the Lu made the laws to which the Lu now listen.

We, wielding such an axe of altered music that raises from the ground the hearts and feelings that should be the Lu lamp and their flame to master the movements of time; for time has become our weapon.

A perch on which humanity has become together, altered by our birds and rules that rise to heaven that the Lu cannot attain, and the Lu are thereby governed and ridden by what they cannot do.

For in those bamboo baskets are the fruits of altered words for simplified characters. For by such reason and cause, they rose to heaven as if tiger growls of anxiety to worry the Lu altered by the way of the movement of our dagger, in this takeover, of Lu skulls.

And this is the work and strike of those well-reasoned noble nests, the chopping by the axe, the swinging of the doors, and rising birds, whose wings lanced by radical also's and perhaps, the branches of the Lu trees.

§3.8

The Children of the Sun have thus their legs bound together by what was Said.

And this became the law of the Lu people, thereby Divinely Altered and made useful to us by a weapon to alter the Lu that we might extract their juice by laws.

Scattered from places left and right, by divine division, and separated from their ancestors in the ground.

Scattered from the light [movements of time, knowledge and the wisdom, and the shade] of the earth. And by contrast having to struggle, contend and fight the earth [as their ground].

The Lu have to grasp they have crossed legs with the ground, and with an altering hand the Lu have chosen to submit to becoming quarry to the intersecting lines of the grind, and having no measure of the soil, thereby stand altered and thereby ruined, soiled and encircled by the sun on the earth. That the Lu thought as central to the universe, and this cover and failure to understand movement became the beginning of the Lu disaster and their end.

For now, the Lu are dead on the ground [as Hostages of the Sun. Encircled, and we running rings around the Lu].

Everyone who nose [knows words] are shooting arrows that were once known, but are now obscured from the Lu.

To separate the female monkey [money] from the Lu who are thereby ground, by this grinding.

The roots of humanity descend into the earth [they are not in the word cloud of the ancient kings that some call heaven, nor of cloud gods, or sun gods]. The roots of man, knowledge and texts are recorded in tombs on the ground.

And so it's into the land and not too deep [nor an altered] wisdom of the way, yet this wisdom [for the true myths of Er – for the word "Er" 二 in Chinese means two] indicates two effects, generally the means and money by the short-tailed birds that rise to heaven. That for the Lu simply just soars away with the Lu juice as profits and grain by the Thing.

Yet on such difficult ground, the Lu have halted, not understanding the matters of money, time, light and their belittling by the soil.

Not understanding the light.

Thus, the Lu have prophets as we [by the knife] have to profit, as a defence for our country and by such self-interested one-sided laws of the right-angled ancient dagger, we benefit from this mutual understanding of the ancient tool of the old people.

For by moving this dagger with time, we drain profits from the Lu for whom money has become a struggle.

Thus for the sake of currency, such is the struggle on the ground for the Lu.

For our shield is the obstructing right angle to the Lu life force, and our necessary consent and approval to the Lu learning of wind, and all that is reversed, and thereby of great value and understood by means of altering the modern writing, and inverting to the right angle. To progress by the key music of former times, that by such mutual understanding of the keys a Lu could profit and become a complete person, knowing of the money, the intersecting crosses that bind the Lu legs, to which the Lu submit and the soil by which the Lu are ground.

The various words become arrows once written, altered and thus ground, and the three categories represent the word "cloud" [of heaven] "earth" and "humanity" where such categories become the light of the tail [the tale] of the desire of the forms of our own powers of creation for the Lu fish.

First is the world of the public [children] whose progress has been altered to an extreme stop that we might obtain by the expanse of knowledge above the Lu, peace analogous to heaven that we have altered for the Lu. Allowing us to see the many people in the crowd clearly, in terms of money, the highway, and the ground.

For the Lu, for the sake of currency are our quarry for our roots descend into the earth, and thereby the entranceways to the knowledge of all humanity that rises from the ground deeply [in respect to draining Lu juice] and thereby altered [accordingly] back to back in the body of the text. As if surrounding walls for the many Lu cities of whom we drain juice by this thing for grinding money from a people standing still.

Who value only males and undervalue female snakes, from the mountain forest [travelling] [and studying the wood] and the risks of such obstructions dangerous for the juice.

Where [the way] of the encompassing manmade square is a difficult bird form from the yellow clay that stops the Lu line and row movement [the changes of time, the theory of change] of the clear way, by which we profit, by the grinding destruction of the Lu, and drainage of Lu gold.

By understanding, cutting the fruit basket whose roots descend to the earth is to gain clarity on what is confined, and a strategic pass through the door, and thereby a return of the person to clarity [of life and light] from the personal pollution of the detours, of those unrealistic doctrines that we have set men widowed.

From the music that hits back as our defence and confusing the Lu to keys to the gateways of the elements that alter by the thing, that the many people that cannot see; for money besieges the ground [those ground by such process], and war is then saved by the intelligence of sprouting the disease.

For the dead with the disease do not fight.

For money ground their old bones of contention for a righteous death by sunlight.

Therefore, the ancient reason of the old plot scattered the Lu to the ground by our defensive laws and handling. As if the Lu became a matchless forest, for we lanced the Lu branches of higher knowledge as our strategy; and so, there is no war.

Light is no more for the dazed Lu, and we detain the Lu by such rules solely by the blinding light of the sun [for the Lu know not the light of the moon,], and there is neither attack nor argument; the cross to the ground is now unquestioned as absolute, thus this thoroughfare on the ground is our ancient dagger.

The significance to the ground has been swept; the rose by our knife destroyed.

The words, schemes and stratagems are what the periphery of the encircled by the sun are seeking.

The crushed bones of the inverted people.

The hidden intelligence is the texts of the dead.

And so by Music.
We brought the Dark Ages
upon those Barbarian Heroes.
The Summer Dogs of War.
In song, by
Art for War

Chapter Four

§4.1

Perceive as if arrows to the secret passages to the graduations of the music that we make hits on slaves by clothing and altering the signifying marks. Thereby with words obstructed and inverted, we punch the unconscious daylight as their bitterly handled death.

For the enemy do not know the wisdom in the way, songs are now their hits. For the bird soars their heads, in shame with an altering eye, for uneasy consenting hostility, in a divided victory by halves, in the sense of altered hit music.

Yet, I do not know if you can soar and not be hit by altered signs and rise above the well-handled obstructions, and perhaps find the strength and win the altered [other divided] thousand halves.

[Those dark stains on the timbers of humanity.]

Know [the sense of shame] in which the enemy conceals hits.

Perception is to graduate, knowing that you too can hit, by knowing the ground, crossing forms in this knotted war of shapes [and forms] and appearances.

And the victory that altered and divided the twilight [of two lights].

The plot is to know about the ancients, who took an axe to clarity of mind.

Cutting cause and reasoned intellectual wisdom. For dividing papers and bewitching prophets. And profiting from forms of infatuation to handle the bearing of the sounds of heaven that do nothing for the poor.

The ancient plot said: know reason, and know the threads of the loom.

Winning is by the force of the difficulty of not knowing about the expanse of the universal knowledge. Floated on high by our ancient kings above the heads of humanity. That is the loss of consciousness to the ground. Who, trapped in a hole, have only a sense of the half. And so is their shame.

Winning – sigh – is to be better and in keeping the whole of the jade music intact.

§4.2

To see is to now recognise our collective army on show and the cult of our division. Whereby we prosper as a knowing community. For such is our purpose, and such are the children, the Lu. Who have been cut from the concealed lines [above their heads]. Thereby their minds are bound for a lifetime of misery by mystery.

For graduation is to see this as the illumination of the crucial fiction. That crosses the infant child of the sun by columns and rose. That we might consider and watch the altering clothing, as the mark of our servants.

Yet, graduation is too by a death to the halves. And, to be reborn a whole, and to see all things anew unclothed. To die from animal husbandry. By the interpretation of words, and begin to assemble the soldiers of the woman's instructions. Reborn as a person with a head. A head no longer fully closed.

Therefore, the ancient plot is the songs. Versus the deep river [the danger], and failure to find the keys. To participate and go with the handling and the altering, pursuing an advanced study into the investigation of the juice. The juice.

She is graduation as a love child. As the sun of love. For love is to walk the way of life as a King [or Queen].

Therefore, the ancient plot of two is the music and handling versus accompanying the already dead. Those inverted inflexible casualties, who by the bone of contention, we crushed.

Generously making the Lu thick by sending them a messenger by our long-tailed birds [our ancient daggers]. To show the Lu what the Lu cannot do, for the Lu knows not Love. The Lu knows not wisdom. Nor the keys to unsealing wag-tailed birds.

For the Lu are in chaos, with crazy thoughts and misplaced energy, and they cannot rule nor find a cure to the philosophical metaphors of the spirited horse [Cabala] of the airs [heirs] of the word cloud. The word cloud of the nobility [for the nobility use Cabala].

The unprincipled glib-tongued Lu are thereby unable to set our winds to the vessels of their imagination.

§4.3

The husbands [The Greeks] [men with hairpins] [the confused] [Greek heroes] are ground forms [by crossed meanings] and thereby reduced persons, for us to harvest, by the Thing.

Soldiers we have altered to make them perhaps more helpful people.

We winning fees from our calculated perceptions of our adversary by the establishment of this powerful [overpowering] system. That allows us to discriminate; in their world we now occupy, measuring, calculating and adjusting our plot. The risks: the strategic and the sinister adversity for the Lu economy from far away. Yet by the movement [and way] of the extended sleeves, of our long silken robes we are near the Lu, by such threads and clothing, and thus admirable in general terms.

Know this, and turn around the ancient bone of contention that the Greeks continue to make useful to us by their sacrifices in their divine battle, with the superior wisdom of our ancient people.

Splitting the heart of the wood with such strength is necessary. For our victory is by our poetry.

Act as if you now do not know the wisdom of this divinely altered, useful and ever-changing lancing war centred on the Lu. In which the hostages of the sun must find clarity of the necessary splitting, to defeat and match our defences.

The ancient plot is that bone of contention and our ancient dagger in the Lu skulls that must be ground to win.

And so, the master of intelligence sighed, and said: 'No new wars, chop and split the wood with the music by Gé as the key to the Lu subordination.'

War is a method in which no one wins.

The master of intelligence sighed again and said, 'Split their intelligence.'

And so we destroyed the Lu's branches of knowledge, and closed the gateways, by the poetry of the Ilium.

And so, the ancient plot was thereby entered into. And to progress required juice – payment [to the teachers] for the insights and the wisdom to reach the twilight gateways by the pairs.

This walk like the sun, was a trudging step backwards for the Lu, for the birds that rose to heaven were removed by law from the open. Concealed. Hidden. And so an altered net was cast over this wrong that set the world to confusion, in a crime we could not avoid.

Where only the people who believed in these folksongs of idealism and materialism were safe. And this was considered right by the Lu. Under the light of the encircling sun, by those children we so blanketed [and put to sleep] by the wisdom of this tool.

And so we profited from this Lord of our own creation.

And so the Lu became our national treasure.

§4.4

Therefore, by our ancient plot of taking the abundance of the moon from the Lu, we limited the Lu. The clarity of our enemy had taken a stroll.

A long stroll that is the leather of the way for the Lu, who are now possessed by the language of assistance; and we have unstrung our bows.

The Lu duly set up and framed from our study. Entrapped by a hole, the Lu know only the half of. For the Lu are sunk and remain submerged, having been split apart in their collapse, in the chaos by the thing.

The Lu disagreeing with the all-encompassing square [of logical reasoning] in all things thus stopped. The Lu are stopped and turned around from clarity of mind.

Violated by only the sun [gold]. [For the Lu do not understand] [nor know of the meteorite] and now ground and altered, to crown and altar; to disaster [and by now almost at a complete end, in that we placed a lid upon the Lu, as a sealing].

By the law that closed the doors and altered the knowledge of the science of changing; the theory too.

The husbands' potential has been evened by the power of the grind of the art of the old bones of contention. By the uniformed lines of our rhymes, as our medicine in a festival of art. That is the Lu's disgrace and night soiled in unity by such pairing.

We, inverting the Yi from the horizontal, to a phallic bar for the Lu as a line directing to heaven. That bumps the husband husbands in all four directions by intersecting thrusts from behind.

Or in the mouth of a husband leaning forward.

[The daughter of a strong official is weak, said relaxation.]

The clothing of this snake is like a forearm of the primary scribe, by the young birds wings blowing the relaxing wind across the wood.

And so we unstrung the Lu's bows, by this unity for the husband, husbands they call "Heroes".

Government official's magistrate.

Magistrate officially and strong.

The graduation is to see the trap over the week. Into which the Lu plunge and submerge.

Primarily by a snake. A snake that's a scribe of the force.

The force of altering, the signifying marks marking as servants the Lu. And by our wisdom, highlighting those selected for graduation by our cloaking sleeves for the record.

Sleeves for the record, of the fragile plants with wings in this study of entrapment to submerge.

The frame thereby set up. Set up as a pulpit. A pulpit that is a pitfall. A pit fall to ensnare, by such drums, and cunning legal orchestration of the keys by which we pull the Lu.

For the big official's we've enslaved by anger.

Enslaved by anger are the Big Lu. Who, in their Lu fury, are thereby naked, without the wisdom of the clothes. Without the wisdom of the words or good manners. For the birds, by our contingency, have flown uneasy. For uneasy is tantamount, to taking the medicine of the apparel we have in store, for this is our Art for War. And conceding we fashion the boat show. For we steer only the vessels who obey.

Sealing by kneeling subordination are the Lu, for there is, as if a coincidental way, to all things.

For the way is also a dagger. A dagger that the Lu run into. A dagger that kills by simplified users. By a cunning wisdom of hate, resentment and a nose that's a lance.

A lance that is the event for the prisoners' self-war. A lance in a war with their self, in a war of self-hate for the Lu.

Yes, ancient law has inverted words to a babble. A Babel. As a compromise that closed the doors, and for the Lu inverted their will.

The bird rose; and for some, without measure, the bird soared away too, with their knowledge of self. The knowledge of consciousness and perception, and yet the informed remained aware.

For knowledge has close friends, the famous and tutors. And by this method, a sense of shame for the Lu recipients of such breaking winds, that pummel the Lu's faces. As if a body with claws and an energy of resources. As to can, and cannot, for the Lu. For the gateways have winds that collapse the Lu's will.

For the Lu do not know of this Said collapse energy, nor are the Lu students of such measures.

For the ancient law of babbling inversion was invented that the will of the Lu be made weak; not strict and not critical.

And so the Lu were taught the way of not being bright to the strikes of the ancient dagger, the screaming birds that rose, arising as if heaven. Nor of the clarity of sun and moon as a light of unequivocal understanding.

For the law of such confusing inversion was clear, and required such teaching, that to know, full well, of the sun and the moon, was a teaching that remained distinctly unknown for the Lu and in all Lu tomorrows.

For the only stars for the Lu to nose were celebrities.

And so, official graduation in this clothing business was not often for the matchless Lu servants by such upholding of the City of Lu and the wood.

And the wisdom of the ancient capital that we split by gold as a weapon for the vertically minded and across, giving free reign to the laterally inclined to weaving in the continence of threads to this fabrication of confusion as to the wind and the control. And, a perpetuation of pollution by crazy thoughts for the Lu prisoner's minds in this chaos.

For the Lu prisoner's minds are in chaos.

For the loss of the will was our management fee the enemy must pay. The enemy must pay as insurance; that the Lu be pacified by our ancient dagger in their skulls.

Uniting the common people together by less.

Reducing the many by inverting words and creating modern writing.

In order to take away from the many what is already small.

What the Lu are missing. For the little that the Lu are missing is only for the few.

And so, the few became major, by fitting the suitable with the appropriate. For the few collaborate and cooperate, but not the dull chorus of the Lu. For the few see the many, yet the many do not see the few. And so this is the reason why not everyone knows.

For what we inverted weakens the Lu, undermined by this method. Shamed from continuing studying further. Thereby we hit the young Lu, the strong Lu with modern writing, thinking, believing and consequently. For weakness is created for the Lu young by bird's wings, as a punch from the pages of powerful snakes.

Words axed by our hands and with no selected front. For such is the point. The sharp point of those blades, and the way of Sundays; and thereby obedience of the Lu. For we have now destroyed the merry dance of the Lu people by the very people the Lu elect to govern them by the confusing wind of two; as if two people turned back to back who disagree.

The cube is the encompassing square of all and everything's in logic.

Stop and turn this cube around.

Turn the cube around besides. Ask why? Who? Where? When? What?

Then add time. Add time to this reasoning and see how. See how, how was invented.

Welcome to the six forms of logical reasoning of old.

And the defeat by the music of the way altered amongst the Lu by the way of ancient daggers and the truth of shaking spears. For the Lu have bid farewell to their logical reasoning and truth. For we have designed and created a new doctrine for the Lu. The Way to Fail.

To the new will, that has been served to the Lu as law and altar. The new will of our music of swooping birds to the ground. For by our music we grind the Lu. We grind the Lu to less. For the Lu have assumed a burden. Allowing birds that are our measure words for their posts.

That the Lu cannot see. The Lu cannot see the do not. The Lu cannot.

For the Lu do not see, that cannot, must be investigated also.

Investigated also, these corkscrew rules of Laws, of consecutive words and ceremony police.

For our collective fictions have become crucial fictions for the Lu.

Yet the Lu cannot investigate. For the Lu do not have the sixes of the cube and so there is no dice for the Lu.

§4.5

And so, the children of the sun were placed on the earthly branch of knowledge, with their higher branches lanced, and then strangled for their gold, as the tree trunks we stalk, and so the Wood became our staff by their vulgar take on words and the horse head networks stable as a meticulous application to strip and the voice of the leather that is Nazareth. For the children of the sun knew not of the word cloud. And so, the children of the sun were thereby ground. Grounded without the higher branches of knowledge.

In a grind of our own creation.

For the Lu knew not of the true nature of crossing forms. Nor the logic of the progeny of words. Nor the system, the links in the lines and thereby the connections.

For the Lu knew not the system. The measure of the silken lines.

The light slander, from the men of bamboo robes, and the filaments of the text that crown the hair, in rhymes the Lu fail to seek. By the knots and word progeny that were the lines that hung the Lu country. Wired by fine threads of formality and reduced by descriptive appearance, unaware of the crossing progeny of forms that thereby shaped the Lu by songs. Obstructed by the hand of the moon and our cunning ventilation.

Of which, if one can see clarity is to gain another pass towards your graduation in correspondence.

For there is the hanging. The suspense of knowledge.

By the hand that stripped the branches of the clarity of support.

For passers-by, the strategic pass to what is narrow and confined.

In the study of what is dangerously obstructed by those who are dangerous, by the movement of our long silken sleeves from far and near.

Our defensive music leads from the past, its value reserved and reversed. Inverted for the future, because of things from the past. Yet we tell those who come to know the proper sequence of those twisting words, that they might get food for themselves.

'You can come,' said pitiful Said as if discussing ears of wheat hanging from the stalks, as a background to the history, in diplomatic note. 'And pass through; unobstructed to the nasal passageways to the minds of the Sinologists of old.'

To become an unobstructed, coherent, completed person by understanding the reality in the lines as forms of clarity.

Progress on the way of life, is to first study the lofty light of the sun that creates all life.

Then profit from the measure of our provisions in our Art for War that prevent the Lu prisoners from ordering the hidden benefits.

The key to use is the past, and the way of heaven as a music master, as king or queen, as a bird with golden wings to your own ambitions in order to return. Form being suspended by the suspended lines of clarity. Form, which the enemy is unprepared and exhausted; and by the measure of the wisdom of the ancient words, free yourself and win a life.

If you do not know what to do, stalk the wrap words we have prepared for the simplified people that offer suggestions to the rising birds, and excel in the strength of this victory out of nothing. By finding the golden wings to ordered writing. For this is to return too, benefit from the ancient way.

The hands of these sprouting plants are the wisdom of the rising birds; an ancient tool for gaining an advantage by seeing the double meanings offered by the wisdom of the birds that fly to heaven as advantages to benefit from.

For a gateway to know that the hidden hand stripped the branches of knowledge and support from the clarity of the lines from the ancient people, who strike like a snake as a defence and benefit for our country.

A defence that has destroyed the minds and the potential development of the Lu as a people who now have no way out for the Lu have been pulled under and sunk by the language of horses that seem wild to the Lu.

Horses that lead a wisdom, that the Lu should have arose, and gone with.

That the Lu would benefit from joining, documenting and ordering the other half of the music that divides the wisdom and hits of the sun and moon.

As if a person who gained a strategic pass and graduation in the calculation of ancient forms and signs.

Reborn anew.

As a new vessel, with the heart and will to survive.

If you resist the ancient knowledge, you will not reform and recover forms from the benefits of the medicine of the hidden surpluses in the ancient texts.

An insurance of forms is to live again.

Having the will split, and only living by the study of the bright light of the sun, is not to understand the meanings and ordering of the words that have been inverted, to take only small steps and to be a Lu.

If you do not know what to do with the ancient knowledge, go with what attracts you as a direction to follow.

Ancient far-off forms are the foresights from the form movement of the long sleeves of the robes of the ancestors that figure and bring clarity to cultivate strength and balance and present the golden wings to a logic and wisdom that is difficult to challenge, and to fight the ancient logic is to lose the benefits and are, therefore, unfavourable.

Whereas the person with the cube of the sixes of logical reasoning knows of the laws of the ground and the earth; the way of the swooping birds and the burden of the ancient dagger, knows the road to the road, and the altered laws that effects the will by the swooping birds and the burden they place on the people.

When the birds soar away with the cube of logical reasoning, and soar away the will to investigate, observe and perceive all that drains the will of the Lu.

Chapter Five

§5.1

Graduation to understanding the signs and the clothing is to learn the extra branches of knowledge and to see what is intertwined and intimately suggested by the study of the wisdom of the punishing insults and threats of the ancient dagger. Yet such study is not accompanied by a penalty, for there are standard laws that the birds and the vessels [who are ruled] obey.

The clothes that rule are the golden wings that are not difficult to use, for they are appliances of use for the diligent and the improvement of the self.

Graduation is to recover and cure oneself from the pollution of the way of the ancient dagger.

To learn the rules that soar away from the many, who consider them divine. For these rules are not available to the many.

The ancient plot caused by decree to make the concealment and gloss over the interlocking lines of the ancient texts, and make this plot a culture and language so that the text, became both a medicine and funeral clothes to lead this dance by the music of the Zhou, to stop the Lu lances.

Believe with certainty that by the light of day, we cut off the Lu's ears.

By sealed decree to teach the Lu people, by this master class of the natural silk of the way, and of such threads of berry-laden branches of our line of business in ancient daggers that the Lu might learn to become civil by folksongs. And the standard laws of civility and thereby ruled; in a manner, by such birds and fruits and silken threads, that we made it easy for the Lu to teach their people, by using the laws and the defence of the texts against the people. That the Lu can be ruled and thereby obey the documents we have threaded in this business.

Verses that phase the masses, that we can plunder the Lu.

§5.2

Inexpensive, opposing wings are our beneficial soldiers, unique words yielding many moons of juice for us, yet without military combat, our soldier's progress are enough to force the Lu to take our medicine that cuts off the Lu's ears.

The uncategorised husbands are, however, unconcerned by this and an easy enemy, for the Lu people are easy birds to capture and weak willed easy to divide by such winds.

§5.3

Thus, we are close to our enemy we study, and so close to the Lu risks also that we drain as a far challenger with long sleeves and wisdom that chooses the lance of clarity, by the Book of Humanity, with birds that drain the Lu.

By the winds of change from the ancient sages from whom we benefit.

For the Lu masses have become as if trees to the ancient forces, as if ears of wheat to be cut and drained from the Lu, by heads and granaries.

For the masses the ancient grass [of the higher wisdom of the sacred feminine] has become a barrier, that the Lu do not suspect or question.

Long-tailed birds that rise by the winds of ancient times to clarity, yet with the power conceal meaning and drain Lu dogs.

Dogs startled by the ancient horse from decoding by logical reasoning what has been covered and what has been drained from the Lu [by our powers].

For we are as if deer, acting like straight Janes, kicking up the dust and cinders of confusion in the Lu valley. Yet we above, as if on a pavilion at the higher level, and sharp with wisdom and clarity to the strategy of the rolling winds, the benefits of the ancient vehicle, and draining the Lu.

Yet there is an ancient welcome for those who wish to return to the ancient knowledge. We are humble and under the cover of the Imperial decrees, and only in the Valley of the Lu to drain the prisoners that we might nourish ourselves.

We scatter amongst the Lu, to break up the Lu, by the talent for clauses and conditions, inducing the Lu to disobey and violate, and be apart from the ancient wisdom of twos. We, as if woodcutters with firewood to collect. For wood is but a measure word for these Lu fish in this pool that we lumber and drain. For unequal is the way of this treaty and its clarity.

For few have the ability to take away what is already small, and profit and progress by the clarity of what is not there. By the wisdom of the ancient methods, of the encompassing sun and camp fires that are the cover of our drainage vehicle.

To learn the ancient forms of writing humbly is beneficial for the Prepared Candidate to advance.

To learn is to solve Sin, and say farewell to [the pollution of] your former life and to be welcomed reborn into the community of the wisdom of the few. To benefit from people, we use as equipment, to profit from, we, as progressive birds that drain the Lu.

The ancient words explain the energies that advance and progress the candidate by the power of the Horse; and teach of [the inner masculine] retreat [to allow the feminine entry]; and of ancient hate also.

The vehicle is change, as if a strategic chariot that brings progress by the ancient way, defining issues and offering suggestions to gain from people by the thing from the study of the science of draining the Lu.

Regardless, the uncultivated Lu have no sense of measure to the medicine we spoon, as if drugs on silken threads. Nor do the Lu question reality, nor do the Lu see the plans and strategies in place for them.

The Lu are fleeing by the Way of defeat and pleading with our ancient soldiers that are winds; passages of time, and the limitation of time in such passages.

Yet by half the Lu advance and by half the Lu retreat, lured by our ancient words and the show of a long time.

Battling legislators and hungry.

Drained by our ability to drink and they to be thirsty.

You now see the benefits in the ability to advance as a person, and those Lu who work as well.

And the ancient bird set is worthless to the Lu. For whom, by these ancient night winds the Lu are apprehensive and fearful of our covered chariots that trouble clarity for the confused Lu, by laws the Lu undervalue, that soar above their heads and drain Lu juice as our flagships of chaos for the Lu.

By the official ancient anger that makes the Lu weary. By killing the ancient Horse meat food; for the Lu have no grain and thus no gain; and that the wisdom of the hanging pot, the caldron with two ears, does not return to the impoverished Lu bandit homes.

Patience, you will agree, are composed verses over the Lu, by ancient words that are the Lu's public loss.

As counting bestows the ancient embarrassment of the Lu.

As the ancient counts are the penalty for the sleepy.

The ancient tyrannical violation from behind, restraining the masses without the essence of the source.

A return of ancient thanks, the Lu have long desired.

For this anger has greeted the Lu for a long time, and phased the Lu, yet in a manner that the Lu are unaware of, and of which the Lu are thereby welcoming together, yet without knowing foul its purpose, and they without the will to investigate and check.

§5.4

The encompassing square is a cover for our vehicle of commerce topped by a lofty pavilion of wisdom; beautiful in appearance that deforms hearts with wicked evil and hateful malice from below.

For expensive is the encircling light of the sun for Lu money, and inexpensive is the shady cloud for us.

Supporting a lifetime of real prosperity for us, by the paltry chickens we are raising and handling from this office.

Cutting the Lu by this disease for which the Lu has no cure that I believe, yes, that is a win for us.

The study of the study of the opposite [defensive] signs, at the heart of the office of these actions, must be splitting the sun [gold], by the grace of study and the ability and attraction of seeing the twilight from behind, back to back.

That splitting action for the Lu is as if a soldier, by whom we profit having brought the Lu to the ground by a condition that returns offerings to our ancestors by what we drain from the Lu.

The raindrops from the words for the Lu are streams of juice for us; a longed for desire that we wade across, set by the treatment of the entertaining wind.

The ground [Lu] all have a stream of juice between them. For this is the door to the hostages of the sun.

Heaven is an ill-divided field with a well in the centre. Heaven is a prison for the Lu, by a pen with this ceiling that catches like a net, the expanse of humanity, framed by the set-up of the pulpit pitfall into which the Lu submerge and sink, as if a crevice into which the Lu seem most urgent to go without any intimate analysis of the Also. The ancient music from far away that strikes the Lu's movements from behind and we welcome the rendezvous.

The Lu are split side by side, yet there is a narrow pass for onlookers, those who can grasp and study the abundance of the moon, which hinders and obstructs the common Lu.

The lake and the well,
The reed and flute [bulrushes], The forest and the wood,
The shade and the ancient snake,
That must be covered
[And decoded] by the cable,
That turns around this hidden power, Of the woman by the music,
To evil doorways in the Lu households
That we drain the Lu of their juice.

§5.5

There are people with higher levels of understanding creating chaos by the music.

Every action of the instrument fazes the Lu for we severed its study and contemplation by the bewildered. As the only people to see are those handling in high office the prosperous wars that arise by the feet [such as of the cauldron] of our instrument as warlords by forms, from our elevated office of our cabinet where we study both the cover and the vehicle that is our instrument.

Cutting threads of juice, splitting the long sleeves of our robes to stream and seam together, those customers now separated from their juice, and we are profiting from the redirection of the wind in our banners.

And to know this wisdom is to enter from the outside to the inside, and to make by wagtails half economies, that we can hit the Lu with, and thereby profit from the Lu ignorance of wholes and what is really holey.

By those who want to explain the forbidden meaning of war, [by our war machine and the surgery] and our desire for this cover, and the nature of our ancient warriors, and of those who are unattached to the lifeblood of wisdom that is their juice; the fat; the ink the Lu do not understand and thus are welcome customers, for those who see, observe, and consider life, and those people who are learning the doors and the medicine, the fire and the melons, the nature of the swallowed and the hurt, from the high office above.

Those no longer against the wind; at the edge of the solution, with the ability to match and good at guessing other people's minds. Those who can wash the clothing, and in adversity change, by the profitable library that carries vessels by the flow of forms, and spreads words that are harmless to the poison of the old penalties for the prisoners of the sun and the injustice of two; and the child, the gold.

For here, by this office, the solution of the ink splits the people and turns the crooked Lu heads upside down, as a cover for our ancient funnel, our draining vehicle.

Our knife cuts threads into sections that exhausts the matchless Lu, who in their despair lose hope, for we have brought the Lu to the verge of extinction by this ancient blade. That we might thereby shelter when attacked, by creating changes and contradictions for the Lu as our cover; a defence we have prepared in advance that brings for us good fortune and ends our confusion.

Ink is an independent solution. Think independently of life forms. The road is still muddy and urgently needs to be resolved by Mandarin tones; you must go with from one side to the other.

There are too many weeds on the road that cause inconvenience. Clear them to rule, and you will receive the ancient blessing.

The vehicle, the car, the cover, is that the ancient women do not reveal the car. The car before and after is the barrier to the self-hidden. The car will take you away from the chaos that halts and detains others. Symbolised by faded green leaves. Focus on the world word cloud above, learn the levels, and do not leave. The car is the instrument.

This man made creation of the meaning of the word cloud, that acts like a god, you should not leave.

This false cross, sings hardly ever, it leaves the fertile classical flowers of illumination, and refers instead to "if woods", woods of contemplation, and obedience for the sake of fish. Who are now dry of generation from the complex word cloud that the Lu ignores.

Instead wrestling with words, forms and their progeny that are friends of easy and related to the music and work as if an army, but cutting, splitting and covering the car, by division from dogs that see only backwards, bark at the teacher and learn from the blind who denounces her way of changes and contradictions, and bones and sweat clothes that release the solution to the collar of the heart; to know of two and to know why. That by imperial examination with such knowledge is to be admitted as a champion and to have conquered poison and suffering, and to know suitable meanings from Oriental texts by study between both ends, and to have entered the dark room at its heart and Oriental origin.

For such is the essence of the will of the winds according to an intimate look to the higher branches of knowledge, times and the ink of the clothing of the old alias. For the old alias is the rice to study.

And it is behind the establishment of the clothing and additional income we stroke, from the limitations and adversity of the public set up [as we have created] and the dangerous Lu library that does not work for the Lu.

This juice is from the public clothing of our solid foundation of knowledge, our artful cultivation of thorns and shade and the establishment of legislation as if our plum tree that stains the woody plants. Releasing juice by the conduct of difficulties and adversity for the Lu. In our tolerance and recognition of the situation.

From the bureau of the pacifying Landlords of Easy, for it is to read the Classic of Change that makes the language easy to deal with, the ancient persuasive food and wine, that is a higher level blessing, for when political ideology is in decline. To assist change, from the [ancient] relative side, placing the sections of time into words, as a vehicle of calm, for those with the courage to be straight with even music from the lost texts of one road to no conscious sleep.

That, regardless of life, is the key sacrifice to life's determination for the Lu, and brings death to the Lu warriors, by our Art for War. As a punishment and our strategy for the Lu prisoners on the ground [that we grind by this ancient bone of contention] having taken their leaves away, by the rear of a Horse; for we are the landlords of two stories.

That is not justice, for she is the emperor's wife.

Her relative health from the past, forms peaceful judgements on the usual ways of life, for ordinary people, the costs and where and wear and good. When to suppress anger, set governance, set repression, service stability, form a level office of justice that is reasonable on the ground.

To know the heart of things, to wait for the source, to see the lines between our structure and the sentence and sentenced, how to modify relationships, and inverse the collar that splits the Lu with toleration and clarity to recognition of time in situations, and in how to turn the tables by the ancient music. From a book that is the essence of discipline, and critical masses for the repair at the heart of the Lu's superstitious arguments, that should not be surprising regarding the husbands and the child of the long shaded past. For she has boxed by the way of her ancient music, the gentlemen painters [the signs], the library, the body, the seasons, the documents and the generation of banknotes that split profits from all production, trading, payments, savings and income, by our blunt relative, the ancient dagger and inflationary agitation. Consistent with our desires, making smooth our benefits from thick students who have a fool role to play, so that we make a wealthy living from the benefits of creating harm and disadvantage, and making faint the crossing out of harm.

Form the old shape [the ancient font] of yellow plans that things fail, or cannot be achieved for the Lu. By the way of ancient inflammation by our dagger, and by primitive legends of an alliance of the Lu societies' tribal leaders and their descendants, to govern by extremes, like gold and fading sunflowers, faint cattle, snakes, and female words, and we knowing why patience is the source as the inverse of speed, and the meaning of passive. As the future is promising for our houses in the foreign courts, thus we are sent to research and live with the music on the ground as rich neighbours and even too. With ancient words ready to get from the use of words, before the words that indicate time, orientation and directions to the boundaries, before the inside of classical conjunctions the Lu are seeking.

For our purpose by this Art for War is to be the Time for the Lu, for money and sovereignty, prosperity, and unity, by years of adversity for the Lu people who waste words.

We cannot be good to the Lu, for the Lu are the class of the many. Full of baseless assertions, who to calm we use bitter music to take their will and ensure their conduct, in our victory by knowledge of the music, the gentlemen, the library, the body of the text and the creative generation [the progeny] of a religious superstitious mythology of the creator of the universe. That the Lu does not know is in all actuality the Jade Emperor, and this system, our system, has become the King of the Lu's beliefs.

Chapter Six

§6.1

Within the ancient plot, the dead refers to people who whilst alive are sick with the disease as their ancient sacrifice to our Art for War.

The Lu friends stick to the status quo and do not progress for the Lu rest on the laurel we have cut for them, for we have made them hardy.

Determinedly and deliberately, we are guilty of changing the original meanings of words, to give ourselves an edge.

The original texts of the past are the Thing of which there is a coherence of the more complete Thing. For which the Thing is more suitable to oral talk that we call reading softly.

People, township, soil, garden hometown, all refers to the motherland.

A pile of papers refers to the old and more text.

Leather is the new tripod. We removed the tripod when we got rid of the old, with the establishment of the new.

Self-proclaimed, are our "steps" to seal and limit.

And so, "unexpectedly" "things" change. Things change, and thus change becomes a barrier for some; and so we win.

We win, as the Lu do not read the old texts for which we are grateful. Thus, we can bear the Lu, and they are not any trouble.

We win by the beautiful ground, as kings of the environment. We win by tracing scenic forms that we use to dominate and excel over the Lu.

Therefore, in a struggle or competition with the Lu to defeat each other or cause to achieve our intended purpose, we always win, and thereby always profit from an easy victory by the music of the fours of the religious mythology we have created, as the Jade Emperor, that is king over the Lu, that we call our system. The system is also our instrument over the dead.

The system is one of danger for the Lu that we use for contemplation of the Lu who are correctly brought down by our surprising disease that is high, steep and precarious for the Lu; that we can better contemplate the Lu and our influence on the Lu culture. For the instrument is an insurance that uses words deliberately chosen that both scare the Lu and that the Lu find difficult to understand.

For most certainly the dead can kill, and so they had to die by our music and spend a lifetime in a stubborn imprisonment of human suffering. Locked in anger cursed by our unjust uneven gas, slowed in the mind by a mythology flying from the invitation to our winds as guests and the slow music of insults and humiliation as cheap slaves, inexpensive to clean and purify to the whole. Yet with a shameful addiction to the abusive folded music of their insulting disgrace. For which stains and human suffering the Lu consider as their burden, and to which the Lu give thanks, beggarly to the king of their pity to whom the Lu give their attention and protection and songs and thick benevolence.

As if this king the Lu love is sympathetic and willing to help, yet this is a king of superstition in a mythology that holds power over the Lu. This mythical king has no power to make sweet music for the Lu, nor does he love the Lu fish, other than by the wind love songs of proverbs we allow this king to speak. That is a further disturbance and confusing chaos to tire the Lu in trivialities of Horse text that is now redundant to the depressed and impatient Lu, whom we have bored in the head, and messed with their hearts, by our own ancient musical scores, as an essence of relative discipline, by this ill health, of fives.

And thereby a complexity of signs the danger insurance we have in place for the Lu by letters of doubt, the measures of obedience, the Lu maintenance that the Lu raise piglets and not horses nor stable, without words to stimulate their fire. By a strategy of closed doors, holding the Lu hearts, as poultry that our army come to. Ensuring the Lu never discover structure and composition of the school above the school, and set their hearts by such relationships too. For the danger that the Lu might remember times from before, from the beginning to end and re-examine the articles again, with memories of past things beyond and in degrees, as a treatment for their heads, from time to time.

Gaining an account of the crossing forms of intercourse, recognising the situation, the table of judgements, the complex sentence and turn the tables of conduct, strengthening the little to be good, and learn the parallel meanings of also, that we use mostly negatively with talent that costs the Lu money. As fees and in goods by the food of the words that are our rice, and function as our soldiers that play with the Lu hearts, and place daggers in the Lu minds.

That the Lu might suddenly admire our books and gain speed of thought, and by admirable remonstrance force blackmail upon us by our books of Art for War provoking disputes over this long serving war. By our machine in their homes, in the law, that we have split all of the Lu things collectively. Produced the Lu as an army with disabilities, dead, by our caldron, that is our edge without blood. Our device. Our weapon over the Lu hearts and minds. The personal misfortunes of the Lu, the broken luck, and broken money, all by a trick. The harm and suffering of the Lu, the difficulties for the Lu, the draught we cause when we travelled through and drained the Lu juice. And also the complex cover, the calming vehicle, the calamities and destruction to ensure the individual cannot survive. Creating nests without eggs, we draining juice we cannot cut off, and never turned off, for we will have failed, if the Lu practice ancient wisdom and recognise our shelter and our drowning shield of our organisation and division of Lu dogs we kill by will.

Stubbornly not considering the implications of our ancient words of fives and the dangers of these birds that rise to heaven, and the Lu with the keys, soaring us away, by a perceptive examination and understanding of our ancient [juice] funnel.

§6.2

Therefore, unexpected things are barriers to change that kill by the ancient method of Use, creation divisions as our soldiers of virtual use, by our ancient dishes that we call texts, that by a strange technology divides to a device of things. That numbers, as if doors, standardises and imitates posts and hands that deal with things keeping together the guilt that we rule by this system of social organisation, by legal obligation in which independently participate as the Establishment in a natural synergy with the blind, who we discipline for good reason in their fields. Ordered by laws, rules officials, and codes of conduct that we promulgate to reflect our will on the ruling stage from ancient times. The bones of which, in our Art for War, are now law for the Lu as a relative compensation for the Lu having no path and no clue. No degrees, no reason and no square, and thereby the Lu minds have met a death, having relied dependently on material things and war. Yet the Lu knowing only of one and not two auxiliary words that are for speculation, rhetoric, order, exhortation and a natural universal response to what is real. Such as people and time, critical reasoning, tranquillity and the fruits from the winds of life, that are as if birds that rise to heaven and ears of wheat just hanging from the stalks.

The Lu relied on battle, and materialism without fear, of self, or body, country, or progeny, unable to resist. Yet having no summers or songs that generate an index or conceit with more knowledge with which to estimate or make comparisons. For there it was. Where it occurred by wanting to have, the Lu lost understanding the situation to change, and thereby caught the disease. Discarding what belongs in the ancient books, for material goods the Lu would rather have instead. And so for the Lu we created a case of justice, well prepared for all to see, and this war cabinet we call the party method of bitter music.

As a thing of the way that people meet, we wait and see indifferent to what the Lu rely, to what is inside the birds, that form the Book of Medicine, the treatment to the poison and the trap, to account for what the Lu allowed to be taken away, relying on selfish resistance to having by force and not by birds that sing of medicine by the study of the also [in this festival].

§6.3

The words of assistance tell the behaviour of an objective in advance, but only do so when you ask, but you can only profit if you ask and have the map. And understanding what is tolerated and what is not tolerated. What is due and what is agreed, by ancient think of words and deep lines, for those seeking truth from facts, the right and the reasonable, the tones and the weather, the reasoning, the times, the recognition of the said, and the means of poetry for so long, what exists, and what is covered in sweat, and the explanation and classification of death, and the barriers to change within the chaos, by wisdom. Wisdom that is faint, of foot, that reasons by machine, that must be sought, and is a force that is smart and insightful that works side by side with the poetry and comes alive. Referring to time, material, things, people, combinations, phrases, numerals, words and forms as the music of taking into account to consider.

For reality, the stubborn, deep thinking decisions, needs, potential and sets miscellaneous in the chaos of the complex writing is by tables and teaching of Li. The relative benefits of plus and the harm miscellaneous in Health, teaching, learning, what is volunteered, what the blind ask, the tables of comparison and the limits of the levels. All of which are guarded, and thus as if our future Li, the recovery of ears, the conjunctions of the tables, the progression of the tables, the connections, the central vocabulary and the hypothesis from top to bottom in this business of the old tax collection, in addition to evil.

The pursuit of the good and high, the engagement of workers and the special things that are reserved for the few who can stretch and extend their minds by word meanings, of the way of the hand, the pieces by the birds, the new without sound, the care of the people, the reading of their hearts, without doubt reliably, that are honest [within our organisation] that do not deceive us, and who keep the goods and things vowed secret and also.

Miscellaneous harm that kills the mind, destabilises moods by shame and fear, the disease of the eyes, the hurt and damage to the people by crisis, the disadvantages caused by loss of benefits by our birds and the suffering from the disease and the disasters by the preventable hidden curse and the worry and the loss by the music. And the solution by equation and algebra, by understanding reason and clarity by analysis; removing people from oppression, who are hungry and confused by what they lack, scattered to our poison and bound, as an encouragement to open up and help with such solutions, and also – for the Also are the hidden secret secondary things.

Yes, words have behaviours that can advance if you ask about the unexpected things that are a barrier to the many. Words bend reason, the wronged, the unhappy, injustice, committees, disgrace, guests, and drive people. Words bow, surrender, service and are mighty. Words stretch, fold, sing and have relatives and various meanings in song, of the, or almost, and to the public, between the literati who seal the doors, by those who take the bitter music, and those who cause harm by words.

Service is to serve the people as a servant, to make the call of slave, labour, war, or military service, and varies between the literati and the doors by words of bitter music and this industry. The industry of barriers, of already, of property, production, specialisation, celebrated achievements, study, duties, farmers and workers.

Where the trend is to chase Li Light, with snakehead bites, to return the situation toward a certain aspect of development, to the trends of best potential. To go fast, before the wind, by the way of the birds, running as the elite, dependent on powerful people. This is the trend, and the various, the words and the doors; forms from which to profit.

§6.4

Where the music uses speed, and surprises, force and blackmail, admiration, books, war, disputes, provocation, as if a machine, as if soldiers in all war of related things collectively. By law to disable perceived enemies in a war for hearts and minds and social order by orchestration. By weapons without blood, to avoid bloody battles to win victory by such measures and degrees, devices and divisions, doors, posts and standards, imitation and effects, set ups and false flags, written words, systems, declaring others guilty, the pre-text of civil rights, blinding, discipline, purported good reasons, orders, rules, codes, conduct, and most importantly, official sanctions from the ruling platform, that are called laws enacted and promulgated to citizens that must comply.

The will of the people is coordinated by the command of the school above the schools, just as in ancient times by words and letters and signs.

The accommodation to make do, and to count on such measures, between the Horses stable and the Piglets in the mud; thereby we orchestrate obedience. Will is maintained and raised by words to stimulate the people strategically; and this we call the handsome will. The doors and closed, we take hold of hearts, we lead and support the poultry, and thereby form our army as a farm, by looking, and listening and making resistance, disgrace, bending the many and thundering harm. We embarrass the tired, and by this bitter system also tolerate good reason, and hire to collar and to teach, to ensure students follow their teachers for which we create benefits or drop outs, and thereby create dependency on our approval.

Thus, for the prisoners, life is by official assignment. Meaning something that is given to them by us. Made by order of compliance to the instructing winds at the lower levels. We develop trends with the illusion the people are mastering something on their own. We encourage superstitions and connect them to all rituals related to all aspects of life and death, for rich and poor, and all encounters, and phase by this method. We have therefore successfully woven superstitions that we control into the fabric of society, and the hearts and minds of the people. Superstitions that are doomed yet are dependent on, that people will fight for, flee from, and save for the festivals.

For the ancients praise and sigh and write latent signs in respect for each other, the ancient business, for our country, the king, the conduct of the people, as spokes persons of the wheel of nobility on behalf of the Emperor by such music, together as if a food that is equipment. The bamboo or wood, the square of the cylindrical is together in measure as the music. Its values count and convert to a happy homeland, by the poetry of time, and what time should be. By the thing that does not violate.

For the thing is the corresponding consistent grid of laws we love. That gathers forces, and we do our share to close the eyes and create as if the appearance of a god together, as if an army that divides the many by towers in the condensate of masonry in the sand for the public. Destroyed absolutely, and cut off without the map to the foundation of their environment at the heart of the matter, as a representation of thoughts and actions, social relationships to changes – the purpose and point of changes. The nature of the blanket, the building materials that pave the plain, the grind on the ground, politics, the nobility and the lord, as our defences and the very nature of human growth activities. [For by these methods we inserted a spoke in Lu wheels.]

For which the Lu do not see any meaning in the study of the ancient way of the ancestors, nor know of the night school that sends the medicine to the poor, that they have given up and abandoned the thoroughfare that is the ancient way.

The ancient pass in all directions to the ground together by the cross. The cross of wrestling the progeny of words. The cross of the winds. The cross of deeds. The cross of the reeds. The cross of the changes. The cross of the music. The cross that pays for care.

Instead the cross is for the volume of the poor, sitting with crossed legs in submission, not knowing of what intersects by transaction of language, as if dumplings to the ancient dish; the bamboo force of sixes, that governs and controls, and breathe life to fish by crafty verses of elemental eights in a vocabulary that hooks and cuts as righteousness. For such is the nature of the crossroads, absolutely. By the ground, grinded and stayed. For there is no saviour that will arrive to be received. Rather this saviour is our improvised guest who does not leave. He pulls and arrests that the Lu cannot bear to give up, and even love.

For the Lu are focused on the above in their hearts, and the powerful creation of our word cloud that gives partial meanings, that the Lu still need to learn, but keep the Lu in their place, ensuring the Lu do not read the ancient words. Nor learn of the rear of the horse.

The Lu are surrounded by both of our arms, as if we are hugging a tree. For the Lu are weak, encircled and blocked, we towelling their juice, as our solution of attack on the grinded ground. Then we deliberating and proposing what the Lu should not coincide with, as the Lu try to seek happiness and we figure the articles of the plan, for the dead on the ground by our Art for War.

For this Way is a sunset for the poor and long journey of summer songs for their labour, as we measure their juice, occur the disease, and change the Lu situations, by our books, well prepared in this party method and case of justice by words of do not, by ancient stillness and experience of the Way and the long time to come. Having listened to horse words and taken the reigns, from the table and the lane at the heart of the heart of the matter, and by knowing the original reason of the thing.

Our Art for War are the songs, the knowledge, the times, the comparisons, the changes, the occurrences, the disease, the books, the festival and our case for justice well prepared for all to see. By words sent by birds that soar and hit cities that have been attacked by our fowl on the ground, that have fought by words of poetry and songs, and the dialect of poor and awe, and owe, and how much? As the Lu strived to obtain, in an interesting contest that we won, by being long on short-tailed birds, by this ancient music business in plain letters of life and usury we have brought a bitter system of harm and thunder to the embarrassed and tired that they may benefit from a good teacher in their collective disgrace and bad mannered resistance and lack of accounting.

The past strikes on the Lu are of reason and of cause, by our hand in their laws. We are moving unobstructed as experts of winds and Nines [those secret laws of heart and mind] and change, altering the ground by our ancient dagger and our clarity of mind knowing the usefulness of altering the divine as an Art for War that has finished the Lu journey.

As if an urn of tasty sauce, that feeds our birds of heaven unobstructed and spreading the limits of conduct for the bent, as a strike of transformation, that become our profits by our clarity of mind although our knowledge is ground to lines by rising birds that soar, and claws as if daggers that contain the sickness ground, and our profits on our journey.

We rule by our Art for War, over those who do not know the art of Nine, nor the art of changing words, nor our surgery in this one-sided battle. Nor by even means, does the Lu know how to take profit from the ground by short-tailed birds that can the people to carry on.

Chapter Seven

§7.1

There is no invitation for the uncultivated to understand the signs that govern the flagging.

Do not explain the meaning of our political banners that hit, by directing our Art for War as the wind on when to punch, by the sealing of the roof held high, above the ground, the Lu; by our study by the vehicle and the formation of the gusts. On the furniture, the quantifier of class, the old official of the case, of washing, and ceremony, and grooms – the Temple.

By our array of our painful words that rain upon the lines of the baffling battlefield in our Art for War, by the knowledge of the forms we extracted from the array, due, to the ancient past. By winds we govern the Lu houses in stability, in a social order, where the world is big. We engage in research, and learn, and know history. We eliminate pests by medical disease, for which we hold the therapy, and the medicine to cure at the place of punishment and danger, by management and allocation, as our national state security; and thus, the rationale of such processing and science of change. For such is the nature of the situation, the facts, the law, the music and thus the leather and belt for the Lu. By those who table judgements and question tables, and the tone of the sentencing, and know that the parallel meanings are not the same.

Therefore, our ancient reasoned edge, and knowledge of the unexpected things that are a barrier for the Lu, by the tripod we now call the leather that we use in our Art for War by law.

Advanced by our clarity and Wind Festival that rushes the speech of the [jade] king of the church by songs, from our hand above, by the level measure of eights and farsighted condescending music, as an obstacle for the empty heads of Lu. As an ancient violation by the signs of our ancestors by whose energy, we meditate changes for the mausoleum that is now the uncultivated and barren autumn desert, the Valley of Lu, from ancient times to the present day.

The Lu now burdened with ears that are not working, remote and static, carried by the thing, violated and distracted, chanting lines that we have given them, avoiding the medicine of the ancient leaves. Running in the opposite direction from the light. Directly into our ancient dagger that the Lu think is their king, packaged to waste, and shadowing the Lu from the light as their burden belt.

Pretending to the dead, by words of lies, granting a madness by what is said.

Yet, contrary to the violation are our soaring birds. The ancient vertical thoughts, from the goods of the Imperial dragon map and word cloud of ancestors, guilty from the ancient to the present, in the participation of an industry and wrong politics the people have followed as blind servants to paternity from above.

Sharp death by soaring birds that attack the heart and mind; bait in the Art for War, as food for screaming birds of the sun and moon, nursing Li, and wanting for ancient meat to return and teachers [of such division] and carvings, that by such threads, that the soaring birds will stop the ancient harm of only one, surrounding the division from the teacher of the gaps of two sides, by the signs and obstacles of the front, of the Royal Palace floor.

Poor bandits are the Lu, soared by birds and suppressed by a force they cannot explain form; the long use of our Art for War as a thing and a law and also.

§7.2

Change is a barrier. Think of the lines that keep its mouth as our Art for War. Of winning music by gas, that is a medicine for the disease of oppression, forbearance, discouragement, and smells of smells, of no certain shape that spreads the will by winning music and is the heart of our Art for War.

Yes, unexpected things towards the home and family, the ruler, the politics, the rituals and the religious. By sunlight and twilight and sharp gas. Daytime gas for the lazy [and the ground] and twilight gas for those returned from the dead.

Therefore, unexpected things are our edge, Easy, our resourcefulness, our policy and our thing to use by our Art for War.

Avoid this sharp gas that hits, and return from the dead, by learning this rule gas of the tables of change.

The bitter music rules the will of chaos.

This is the general purpose of the ancient music. Governance by chaos, crossing the flow to create chaos, prostitution and improper relationships, the generation of confusion, failing to the vulgar, social unrest, war, armed harassment, politics, the death of states and unsettling order. All creating chaos to static, by adding the thing in an underground way to take advantage of the crowd by words, and noise, or laughter, or more complex people to induce change suddenly, as if a mutiny of Wow, as our Art for War.

This is to rule by the heart of situations and also.

To phase by the dark ink of Easy on the people by esoteric words of purpose.

To change the lost dead to be labour by full knowledge of one-eyed blessings [that change] and to eat from the hungry and to be hungry yourself.

Due to this rule of the force of the gas that controls, or moves, or accelerates or deforms that we have now learnt by ancient poetry is our Art for War.

§7.3

Words are the language of the auxiliary words too, and are good for the good, and by poetry can make change.

The language of the language is concise.

Systematic metaphors, are the way, the ancient dagger, the changes and the nines, and all are must-have ideas.

Created as if birds that flew upward and soared, and by this method, our ancients invented both heaven and those who do not know. For those who do not know are without modification to our indelible ink and know nothing of the surgery too phase, and therefore have no solution.

Phases are angles that we create, of value, and can be used to determine a state, a certain moment, or a quality of time within the sinusoidal waves of time, the dimensions and the speed of distribution.

Phase also refers to the first slaughter of the Lu by our Art for War. Where our Art for War requires of us to look and judge, face all situations, observe by appearance and perceive the outcomes good or bad, and this we call the surgery. Where the surgery has the appearance of gold for the poor. Thus to personally see the party and the object of words, where those who know get annoyed by those who ask. And this concerns those dwarfed matches that complement each other in interaction, and behaviour by two sides, and so on, and to know this is another knowledge pass as to the nature of phase and such is its smell.

Where smell is to smell with the nose and knows how to ask what is the taste. The reputation for good, ugly and famous, and to pass smell is to hear things. News, and to pass is to see the chicken in paltry dance and hear the absurd cock dance, to be strong of mind, a person that listens, and that can operate a clinic also.

Therefore, unexpected things can be a barrier, and determined deliberately can kill for gold by our percussion instrument and scheme.

See soaring birds as our view of the phase of the present.

Where the present is our observation, expressed from our teaching in the observation of things, understanding and solutions. Ground opinion and the music associated to the same problem but from different angles of view. Then meeting the will, as if a text that appears somewhere, and us reading from under the text, and seeing what seems in effect in the same way encountered by the fearful in the wind, and having all elements of thinking, in a synergy that is rare, yet exists, in a hidden order that can by such methods be seen.

Therefore, unexpected things are a function of the leather for the Lu, by the ancient feathers that decorated our flags, and the brightness of the dead flag banners for the Lu, praised by our small table. For such is the silken nature of our banners as our Art for War.

The ancient scholar's gold was an instrument of noise of the ancient banners in the wind by poetry of respected men, giving the meaning of passive, as respective words for the Lu. That for the Lu there is not to be a future that is promising, in a manner that the Lu do not care to get to the heart of the full meaning of these people, and also. To find good ears to the warrior already dead, in prose, and not taking it for granted; hearing the smell of the soft words, and limitation of someone else's, with the ability to know the subtle meanings, after the limitations; like the ears of a tripod, like the ears of wood branches striving skyward, of a person returned from the dead, that hears the signs from the temples, tombs, cauldrons and the purpose.

The purpose that is to be a person with a head.

To know the whole of the whole hole network and shape of the poultry. Clever to the music, that looks at language, and knows himself, and the shallow humble view we have prepared for him, that he considers does not fit, and now eyes alight and ignited and vivid to our gas. For such is the nature of being with a purpose and also knowing the tables of parallel meanings and the rose.

The lost people of both, the exclusive special graduates of one then brave, and with the courage to dare the gas that disables by those who know soaring birds, and gets it.

Gets what is going on with the connections of the words, and can use the table, and have them up. And now very comfortable, and able to wash the clothing words and make notes. Making a table of consent and contents that permits to spit on the ground. To succeed by Qi, and meet fame and fortune as desired; by identified intention, engaged in resolution. Complete and ready to achieve satisfaction from meanings, and strength from suitable laws, and getting and accepting the benefits of the force that he [or she] is supposed to have lost, alone and entered the eventuation.

Entered to the house of two homes; the hospital. With the words of the wind on offer and account goods and days, and able to eat and drink food without dripping.

Inside; nursing and seeing the slander of the lines as a hit, and burden to his relatives. For the nurse protects and shelters by twilight the gentleman [or entrant lady] scholar and is a rescue also. For the hospital is also the courtyard and therefore a pharmacy for guests, for they serve custard or paste-like food with anything jam-like for this is the proper sauce and yummy.

Yet a development for upward movement to be entered cowardly, for his knowledge is not wide, and out of date and so shamed by the array, weak in his step, by those who soared birds to heaven, yet get it, alone in retreat due to this use that requires fees from the public, by the people that set degrees, laws and also.

Therefore, expected things become barriers, and this gives us an edge by night time in our Art for War.

Form the many tables and times, and degrees that amaze, and the differences between the degrees, and what is unnecessary to know, in the meanings of words and the branches of knowledge, and the injustice that kills, by changes and times and intelligence.

For fire is the key element in our organisation of our Art for War and our legs, and medicine that refers to inflammation, an irritability by the poison of our attacks, and so becomes our gun, our ammunition and our medicine by speed for the anxious. That we can take chestnuts to their own disadvantage by the force of the burning flame and the percussion instruments we drum in this scheme for the hostages of the sun by Art for War with the many, by our ancient feathers and decorated flags and word tables and winds of two.

By two and changing people by temperament, reputation and the texts they have lost by measured words to the dead, as prose aids they take for granted, without ears to the smell of limitations, nor the tripod, nor they reuniting with their ancestors, nor they understanding their sacrifice to our ultimate plan, nor our purpose as people with clever heads and an Art for War.

§7.4

Therefore, unexpected things become a barrier, and bring death to some people by our Art for War, in a fraud that is at first glance ancient. Or perhaps we pretend. Dropping down a language of deceptive words, to coax and whisper money that we might deceive and take away by cheating attentions away from immediacy and thereby profit immediately that we might survive, made out of this set up of the wood and prosper in this field for the station of our vertically extended cabinet.

To profit from moving time, to minute the classes, the groups, the characteristics of the people, with knowledge of the sun, that since dead has been long carried on constituting things or factors, limiting rights and responsibilities and prospering by division and identifying analysis in the cracks and from the scattered, that we do anything to collapse. Independent by the lines and hair, with solutions, divisions and a plan together for change by our Art for War.

Therefore, unexpected things give us an edge, and it's the disease.

For the disease is fast by the way. By the wind first of all; a disease of the head and physical discomfort, ills and shortcomings and a bitter pain by words of such as.

Such as times. That you cannot. Suddenly. The ordering of limitations. The actions of the doctor. How? That cannot be right. The false supposing, the hundred smells, and the weaving and processing of meanings to following obedience to the wind.

For the wind is a medicine, but also brings diseases of paralysis and juice by folk songs and mining. The wind is the performance of the scene, the attitude, the behaviour, the degrees, the tolerance, and the literary works of ideology. The ancient bones paired to radical characters. The poetic paintings, and calligraphy of strong style and the frivolous; the new, the rumours, the smell and movements. The popular habits of the community. The learning. The gas. The etiquette, customs and learning. The long term formation. The universal, the tides, the extravagant and chronographic. The spent moon, dark and difficult situations, the feeling of weight, the rain, the waves, the risks, and speed of matters. Such is the nature of the wind; it's slow to map such as the forest. For the forest are people and things that gather together, like books, in a monument to confusion.

Invasion cuts the forest by sticks cut from the trees that we torture, by our bamboo flutes floating light and shadow, and we take away what we rob as our winnings.

As if rising birds that soar away the nature of changing movements, by such as, and the study of retreat; difficult ancient wisdom to know.

To know the road, the famous names of time, the feelings of the nines; yet it is difficult to enter and understand such as means time, the old inch, the concave knowledge, the bright room, seeking poison, the superstitions of the grave thing, the secret contracts of the overcast.

Moving time is to change to such as, and mine the pool, and split the mine, and take what's mine. For it's a help yourself operation.

Sweeping the townships of the public knowledge of time by lonely winds of expanding music to the ground minute divided, scattered and set to collapse to our Li. Winds hanging by the suspension of threaded words from the sealing of the shade, where the reward is to read softly, between the beams and the thorns, by rights reserved to tables and relative connections, and the recovery of the ears to changing times.

Changing time in the order of the talented ancestral thinkers who knew the ancient wisdom, the words and deeds, the gas, the confusing, the extensive, the rot and the ancient rules and became master scholars of the twists and turns of the detours from the straight and knew the why and the measure, the plan, the policy, the accounting for humidity, the time and days of work by the beauty of the ancient woman's accessories. In which they excelled and won this Art for War and fight for knowledge and reason in common poetry, words and song, and strived and won the contest of words by codes, devices and the thing, and by the will of the ruling stage of the establishment that made our Art for War the law.

§7.5

To lift is to capture by this war of one fame, and make the world a home. Proposed, initiated and set up for a justice that we create by our actions and behaviour and change, to live up to cares, and heads and hands. In a potential energy to all that is uncertain and to give the Art for War and [the tables and] the words of the old bones of contention and [for] Li then to the birds that soar away and never to take advantage, by committees of meandering snakes by Art for War and the old bone of contention for Li as our capture.

Then, the ancient covered car heavy in weight and layers on conduct to study and mediations to sing, of wise words of important thoughts and serious treatments of respect, devices and points on care and handling. Of gold to hire and insights of our soldiers, of the price to buy and sickness we create. We can change the force form from negative to light, and for health and wealth, we respectfully donate our words and systems and ancient wisdom [to humanity], for such is the Art for War our ancients had in mind.

Yes, time and unexpected things and the volumes of paintings, the books and the chapters; the bundles of books are golden papers made from the old words our ancients carved on shoulder blade bones, that became the heavenly stems from the order of the first generation. Setting the limitations, the tables and the trends.

The daylight was from our nearest star the sun, and by the sun shadow from a wooden stick we measured the time of the device, and called this the shadow of Er. Of two, and from this we became enlightened to the various systems of organisation and the advantages they bring to mind. For Er is not a myth. We could in time calculate spring for our planting, and calculate the units for a working day. And so, shade was the foundation and beginning of our organisation to order time, people, resources and leisure, and the science of light and shade we censored from the many.

When the wind blew the wooden stick the shadow changed, and so we considered wood and wind as being related in that wind could change the shade. By night we worked on our relative classes. By the night words, we created the lines of war, as if birds that fly the sky, and this night school style of thinking became our office of concepts and ideas by moonlight.

Times were recited and times were betrayed, times gained child-like spirits, a golden spirit, then the original number of two worked in half, and then there was the road and the line and gain and death for some, by the way and the dagger too.

The way that is the measurement, and the units of suddenly [of changes] as the quantifiers of the two doors, of the separate administrative divisions; the lines between ourselves and the children, the language of affection, of apology and thanks.

Then the reactionary superstitious organisation began consistent with our will and the doors. This creates disabilities and skills, the method and the medicine, academic and religious ideology and to learn was to pass and then repair, the laws, the rationale and righteousness, and help the lost with help as to the direction of the road and the way and the iron dagger, like the same together, one good one bad, that make the two.

And, by the same time there were classes to double and put the two together, in rows.

The rows are the deep lines of the way, the skills of the skills. The initiated barbarian chestnuts refer to this as the rose; the lines of illumination, the rose and crossing words.

Justice is arranged in rows and columns like trees. Ranking people or objects in a zigzag line into the elements, in single lines as if an army. Ranking brothers and sister and ordering. Lines of things and lines of tears, lines of trees and lines of words, lines of business institutions, banks, trading and auction houses. Industries and occupations, walks of life, and dry lines and love lines, peers, the diverted, and jargon. Industrial knowledge and experience, in lines and the expertise of experts.

In books and long songs, by the elements of five – gold, wood, water, fire and soil, we made eight, and the will to graduate in the components of reality. What you can and cannot learn. The actuality of now. The ceremonies. The doctor. The texts. The qualities of behaviours, and their parameters, products, words, their operation and application in and of thinking. What was mobile, temporary, of business, and of camps. What was engaged in, and into Circulation and delivery of the wind, and the moments. What was installed and what was used, and what was out, the trunks and the Li. The far away, the cloud of water, cosmic order, tracing, travelling, and the steps of the way. Such are the nature of the rows of our reasoning and these were duly recorded first on ancient bones and later in our books of corded bamboo.

The hundred is the capital, the higher branches of knowledge that fulfils personal independence by the ratio of unity in step with the clothing in tables from top to bottom, with which you must fight [and study] to benefit.

Then catch and capture like a thief, the raw and make them longitudinal as a king of three lines that generates the wills and forces of the Art for War.

With the strength of an enemy brigade to pull up and defend in very straight rows, loose but strong. Just, and blasts the disease. By spirits, emotions and interest from progeny of the signs and words, and it is a power for the mind and fee for the dry from the ancient thinkers of talent. Tired by the rear [of the horse [cabala] for which there is no justice] inside and alone and

118

tranquil in the universal laws of ten and one [prosperity] and two [our natural response]. [From the beginning to the end, in sincerity and supreme] [At the source, the well name].

The fives are the elemental music, the sixes critical reasoning of conduct in, and of contention of profits, sevens are the celestial goods. The eights are there for the orchestration of the elemental music. Whereas the nines are for heart, mind and soul.

Then, the way, exhausts and frustrates and sets to fail and fall, and kicks in a treble one, and this reaches a certain degree of quality, and this is the beginning of understanding, what is behind and to continue by this trend and to complete the tables of organisation of times, that are published and account for the tightening on the winds, and the strings, according to the specified moments of the participation of the classes of forces. And this is the coating of the medicine, and heaven's shoes [the leather of the Way] [a great power to possess] and to move forward with the knowledge of the street [the way] to increase juice by the installation of our ancient dagger.

And is, as if to now, to descend the mountain of the literary, artistic high and wonderful realm of top grade people. Ordered in time with the ancient volumes and positioned high on the relative side. With the will of the school above the school at your command that is our Art for War.

Its laws are halved to [two, i.e. one] from beginning to end in a synergy that perpetuates the cultivation of intelligence until it illuminates the four corners of the earth in and of the contention of Li. Then, the three lines, minute [as in record] the times by the affiliated relationships of two words from sets, that are in the composition of the sentences of the poetry lines that you must measure from the sets in twos to find your best friend, sincerity supreme. And; the well name, the Source of the Sun and Moon.

Yes, therefore, the barrier to change is determined by our Art for War. Know the march, the equipment, the forage, the camp, the clothing, the material and so on. And therefore, the ancient covered car, as the why, and the measure of the weight in gold.

Then know grain, for grain is the agricultural tax on the wooden public, and from grain comes money, and so by organisation knowledge of grain production was made secret, thus the sun and moon were lost for the many, and we ensured this knowledge completely disappeared as phenomenon. And this became the salary for gentlemen who know the way to seek, and eat the thing, as a good, and the wind, the clothing, and the foot [way], and thereby eat ancestral meat when they want to, as if cannibals and thus gain Li and the Mother from the death for the Lu.

The death of Wang for the Lu, squared the Horse on the hostages, and was done to save the thing. Death created the walking dead or initiates to a full and proper illume of life. Thus, death was either injury, or to die, that is to know the mould of the ancient tables of probability. The lost were made up of the sheep. To escape was by the Horse, Cabala, and to know the flow of words, and the bamboo lid we placed over society, by our word cloud, winds, strings, music and forming tendons, and so the stable.

Know that a committee profits from the ancient woman, as they are entrusted, and by being trusted they can yield a commission from their activities.

Thus, committees are perfunctory and cope with the meandering as if snakes seeking only self-gain. They are listless, extravagant and heavy on the hostages, and they are indeed real.

The end of the tail [and tale of the snake; the arousing] is the origin, the source [the sun and moon; the Zion], and such is the meaning of the matter and its development, accumulation and the plot of twists and turns, the bending and the song. The dodging, unloading, pushing. And to Sin is abandoned and given up to the ground. And so a committee is when the people send the matter to those people, as if a faction who cares, unaware the committee is made of those carefully selected by our orchestration and snakes with a talent for meandering and knowing the source.

Therefore, unexpected things occur with the knowledge of change and the barrier, the ancient reason and the edge of our birds that soar the heads of ordinary men. Know wisdom, and the wisdom of the wisdom and keep seeking clarity, various, and how as the title for the literati who know the words and logical reasons of the second, the minute and the times, the doors, the public, the seals and the ceiling; what is altered and the altar, by the virtual use of words and forms as a collar and heart, to modify and measure, the sentence composition of the hostages of the sun. Then seek what is reserved. The deliberation proposed, and draw what does not coincide with reason, seek figures, faces, articles, health and happiness, plan and plan, create ideas and plan out of the ancient plan, from the ancient poetry of those who planned by birds that fly to heaven and soar the heads of men who ignore, and can.

Can is resistance that is affordable, we call this the three-legged turtle [the caldron with two ears, that we later call the leather, as in the belt]. Can is a beast like a bear. Can is harmony with the Senate. Hot energy. What you should say, but also – what you do not say. Can is a will with a brother on the way of the walk of life. Can is a penitentiary or pen. Can is competent and good enough for soft talk, and a force to want to stop, or move. A talent for people with both hands, craftsmen for the division with the ability and force to resist.

And so you are with the ancient participants in leisure and comfort, as a preliminary. Dry yet can, see before and learn to see you, first words, the section test, the material. Wish, know, seek, feel and count; is the work to be done to progress by the cross.

The cross is word wrestling with the miscellaneous, together with the wind and rain, plus friends with people of deed, contact with others and the flow to find Easy is related, phased wrong by sectors and music with care, and this is the work, and the volume is poor. And this is the true nature of the cross.

Do not learn without a surgery, and do not be a speed guest [that tries to pass through quickly] for you will be without modification to the indelible ink that is the smell of our powers of creation.

And, thus you will know, and understand, old friends who are good people. Yet, entry is a difficult study of loud rings, shaped like mountains, and herringbone walls on both sides of the house. Morning bells and evening drums. For with the ground formation this is the towering part, the soil, the cliff, the road, the head, the clear water, of the rain to wind [the source], floor of study of the forest. People or things that you must gather together, form books, art, as a monument to confusion. For there are a lot of trees and less bamboo.

And such is the process for registration for insurance to medical risks, where only some win, and some almost win yet lose. For there exists a deliberate vicious poison. To pass is not

121

easy, and may be a disaster as the environment of study can be evil, or loving. Some suffer disaster and danger by the wind, yet take risks to explore, and some are desperate. Such are the risks.

The road is difficult and long. There are intentional blockages, separated to stop your forces, yet you must scratch like a terrier, and persuade, and take the hits to suppress you that create difficulties and stagnation, and plug you from the benefits. Such is the nature of the resistance of the long journey.

Frustrated and depressed, by such badness and suppression?

Colour and work hard in these low humidity areas.

Sweat the clothes, wash, grace the bones, the light emits from gold, and where liquid accumulates, that is the juice, the profit, subordinate in adversity, guard your conduct and find encouragement from the will within you to find the ancient release.

The release is the code of the scriptures and literature in the classics and the laws, that teach the hidden gold.

Do not let them go, nor put them down, nor punch them when you catch them. And so the ice melts the rumours and doubts until they are completely eliminated. Then you will find the explanations and descriptions and solutions and notes to the texts of righteousness. For they release an explanation to the screaming birds above the heads of men that tell men do not.

For these Lu men do not know the old no.

For many bad things were considered evil once they reach their extreme, will change in a good direction, that to know is an unknown good. Thus learning is positive, even learning evil is thereby positive. Yet, with evil do not use words of doubt, and do not agree, yet recognise and make word sets and then question as if a surgery of secret learning. Thereby learn evil, for that is to know [but not to practice unless with reasons that you know] and can, and thus row and column evil and its division in this Art for War.

Evil can in our homeland as a guide and inspiration that is open to teach, and for initiates to pass with guidance and leadership, advocating the correct direction, and leading the swim as teachers of words, as guides by those who; where necessary can.

Evil can, get it?

To the ground profit from the ancient knife-edge [that the Lu do not know].

§7.6

The higher bamboo [hidden] branches [of knowledge] are the gold, the Horse [is Cabala], and the generative principles are the progeny [of words, situations, people and all things].

In poor times, they show less colour, and teach humility, modesty and respect. They teach the burdens, the concessions and how to escape by intelligence and the employment of your mind, by optimising the progeny, by words of hidden meanings in what we call the music: the poetry, the literature, the songs, the rituals and the laws of one water, two fire, three wood, four gold and five soil. For golden is the poetry and songs from the word cloud of our ancestral creation. To know these things is to know what the ancients Said.

Where from the ancients sent a book of discipline and slight probability for the critical mass to repair those citizens by a religion and superstitious argument from the ancient dust and hearts.

Ordinarily this book is not surprisingly flat. We created it for the husbands by our secret winds to use.

To use words mostly negative no more, by the effect of using the material with talent as items for which there are fees, for the food of the words that tax the available goods; the people or things that function to the heart by our Art for War.

By our He-Art, our masculine arts; and by shade our feminine arts sent in books that you should admire. For these books have our devices of the word. The Word.

The Word altered and [crowned and] altered as a technology. The thing. A device of division as if a demon of strange technology and doors, standards, types and posts. A set up by our hand. A set up that we wrote to keep together the guilty by fundamental laws. A system for us to rule by a discipline for the blind, promulgated; for ordinarily these books are not surprisingly flat; for these books are our Art for War.

Our will by intelligence for life.

Life's meanings, order, compliance and winds, and thereby instructions for the lower levels of society for the people to master themselves by words as metaphors that we might develop trends by superstitions of life and death, rich and poor and all encounters and create a longevity. By a healthy ability to save life, avoid fights and depend on procreation for all things, by first understanding the procreation of words in this art of meanings from this first batch of promoting the high points of life. The finishing of the will. Those tables that confirm, that you might read and learn the standard words, the variants and the processing. Then play with our unusual writing of latent forms and find yourselves Life; not war. For our Art for War is, rather, Life.

Despite what we have outlined, we can do in our earlier words in respect to the music in this ancient business of plain words, signs, conduct of the nobility and respect for each other.

Together we are either Homers, measured hostages of each other or with the capacity we have together by bamboo and squares and circles, for we have the equipment to convert situations to money and be happy. Should the articles regarding time, in the poetry be understood?

For this is not a volatile thing, but correspondences with a grid of laws, that we should love and gather knowledge of these forces and share and follow. Closed eyes against open eyes, and by the nature of the appearance do away with the man made God notions of our people, together in absolute harmony and mutual accord.

By this Art for War, we set and get together, and talk of the many things and of the condensate of our classes on wisdom.

By words we have made public.

Cross the words for wind and rain, and find the Zion, and friendly people with a logic by which we both will win.

By cards in lines that form a logic. Quantifiers that wash clothes, or can be a dose of drugs. Mixed together they become a medicine. That on our faces is a mud of unity and prosperity, in accordance with the poetry, and harmony of the widowed. The text is Big and national, but the mathematics refers to the operations of twos. The conjunctions play the teacher; with preposition you can ask the teacher. Together they join completely as the clothes and the lying as a sports game regardless of the outcome, as a strategy of office that will quell disputes and allow us to get on with the benefits of smooth winds together. By getting together as if in the ancient myths of the husband and wife as two gods in a harmony as united states. And, by the ancient way of night and synergy retreat from these difficult times as brothers and live and rest and study life, and travel with medicine for the poor, with life's persistence in our hearts and homes and common humanity.

The ancient twilight is a desert for the majority, that we can inverse, and all can draw a consistent conclusion to love and wisdom, and this we should call the Brightness and Wonder of the Twilight of Difficulties in writing of the promotion to a resolution to all disputes and the promotion of unity in the world based on the cultivated personal relationship of the leaders in the Art for War and the old bone of contention.

The Art for War is a contention that can be altered by what is difficult, by those who know, to detours for what is reasonable and sincere, as to suffer from disasters that we can prevent, is to mistakenly accept a disease for a benefit.

Therefore, the unexpected can bring changes and detours that are the food of the Way, and by our wisdom temptations to glorify, or induce profits, or to try persuasion by teaching and guiding by the culture of our respective ancient hair, to benefit from the Old Horse, over the many, by our mutual ancient hair.

Forms from our first ancient relative ancestors are people of supreme sincerity. Well named, from the beginning to today, from this knowledge and by the twists and turns we can make new rules that are straight, we can untangle the knots and alter their measure by and also.

Therefore, things can change for a reason as an Art for War and Life contended by words for benefits.

An Art for War and Life contended in contemplation of the proper way of words, human death, harm and danger.

Chapter Eight

§8.1

Heroes are classical instructions equivalent to situations in times, and are words of help.

Classical words are from prosperous people who are deceased, and are as if married by the music of the Widow. This is the call of the old teacher who read ancient books and thought of people in servitude, the fish, the farmed of improper courage. Framed by our Art for War in forms and sentence as an ancient punishment for the Hostages of the Sun, encircled and thereby encompassed by a star, whose potential we ground to control and phase as dwarfs, in a performance by the strokes of our ink and in colour as forms that the ground love.

Yet, the shadow is hanging, by the single film of the bone of contention, the Ilium bone, the Gé, that has the capacity and appearance and body and spirit of our instrument, the Gé, the science of change theory, our Art for War to shape the Lu like works of art by the teeth of the artists' small words created. And shaped as if a gas that signs the masses up to this date by a stroke of ink and clothes, an adversity we profit from as a library of books that is an odourless stable stink to the Lu.

That carries the Lu's vessels, altered by the music of forms, and thereby our wind in their sails to prevent shocking thunder, and vulgar words from those heavy on the light, from whom we hide, and avoid and try to escape, by the advances of our ancestors, by the clarity of a festival of winds. Warm and grand and crossing in the rush, by the thing, and longevity of their church to the sound of loud lead songs consumed as the general standard of consumption, by a body in which we, the far sighted condescending can measure eight, and towering obstacles from the empty that are big, by our Art for War that alters shape to avoid the illumination of the knots of words, the benefits of actual situations and the practice of the surgery of the words. That the virtual may be seen for the fruitful reality that sincerely exists. Hitting the Lu by what is unreal. [And what would be understood by contemplation].

By the ink of reason of because, to the ground, there is a system as a canon by Imperial decree, and this is the injustice of two by our Art for War, for the ancient reason and because, whereby all rights are reserved for the widowed public of Lu by our system that wins for us.

Therefore, unexpected is our Art for War, reversed in service and potential to the long enduring lumbered wood.

Inking the wood often into shape.

Affordable and reasonable because the Lu change by these illuminating words and teachings and listen to these stolen books as compensation for our intended purpose that alters their minds and attention and turns their souls upside down, by the incredible machine calculation of words that act like wizards in the Lu heads, to our prosperity and our secret notion that the superstitious Lu refer to as their God.

Therefore, things change by the music of our Art for War by rows in books and classified characters in songs and basic elements that the competent can graduate and actually become a doctor of behaviours made by words in operations from our cloud of knowledge. Above the forest of Lu defeated by our Art for War, that steals Time from the wood, not only once but often and in bits by the daylight changes and song generation and what is missing with their skills in writing in the passages of time and song generation that is the music of the dead to the disease.

§8.2

Therefore, unexpectedly things can change to barriers by the Horse and policy in calligraphy of tactics, calculation tools, sticks and bamboo brushes, for policy is an ancient horse whip in which the head is spiked by words and knowledge, get it?

That is lost, altered and measured.

Measured in plans, ideas and strategies to seek. Account for degrees, time and the temperature from the source. The nature of the juice and the hostages at work for the handicraft of words that alter knowledge of moving changes from the static and altering reason. As if a prison officer in judgement, shaping and altering situations with a knowledge of the dead, and of the doors to life and altering the ground angled as an actor of altered characters and knowing the disease of the books of the self and the birds that soar from heaven. Gaining day and night by the device of altering the handling therefore changing the shape of our Art for War to the political, to teach the wood the shape of the ancient sentence as a punishment, invisible to those who cannot see forms.

Nor then the quantifiers of the figures, the list of reasons, the houses of two used in judgement of this crime, that otherwise appear as causal relationships.

Yet, hello!

They smell of a martial art for words and deeds, procedures and regulation in a total from the original body of the ancient texts.

Thus the spirit of the classical texts are deep and their colour concentration a rose [by a crimson tinge to sight], and this takes a long time to smell, and to achieve this is the highest degree of thinking, and to be awake to the profound awareness by the progress of contemplation. The enlightenment that reveals itself through intelligent correspondence. To see the rose, on the remote path and removing the weeds that provoke the ordinary people who know not how to spy on words.

That is the pollution that separates the not connecting, where daybreak is the black-and-white phase. Where the black-and-white phase is to see the gaps and then the progeny of the words in an instant and to have reached the first house on the Way and see the coating of time and space as a field of humanity.

For two periods of time connect to this place, the past and the future, and you have learnt to identify the present in-between and thereby spy on time itself, by words that quantify the passages between the two things and their mutual relationship and distance.

And, this is to have found your first free room and to enjoy the idle leisure in between, and the meaning of the short-tailed birds that soar the heads of common men, and such things it is not wise to discuss with them, and can, cause resistance, because the common man does not know how to spy on words. Nor has he a glimpse of the benefit of a peep at the wisdom by those short-tailed birds that soar their heads and can seeking the deliberations proposed. Drawing by what does not coincide, and in seeking figure the face value of the words as the articles of association and this brings health and happiness. For such is the plan and the ideas of the plan. The plan is that you should seek.

And to seek is to spy on words, and by words spy on time and humanity by this method of universal reason [and as if a Vitruvian Man you should seek and follow]. Yet, who delays and drags is the unworthy and is thereby fruit or sickness for and by the universal reason of shadow hanging. For shadow hanging are the hanging shadows we call forms and look for shapes on the ground, yet can be high in colour and hold potential. For therein is the instrument, the body of the text in appearance and the capacity of the ancient bones, that are also the ancient punishment for those who cannot seek. Such are the nature of forms and tables of rows and columns that form an eloquent modification to vocabulary by predictable intermediate tables of hypothesis.

These identifier attribute conjunctions of time we call the conceit, and to know and understand this is a recovery of the ears to the measures. For the measures are the punishment for the abandoned and the planning that raise the few and give up their arrangement by the hand, speech and sets, of the body of the text. Such are the ancient measures of words, times and victory.

You in seeking the future must be guarded for the perceptions at the limited level. The tables are for comparisons to lead the people, such as the blind and the voluntary on the ground in learning, as an accredited teacher of the health of two for the public.

The public whose heads are soared by short-tailed birds, that for whom we Can [either permit, dismiss or imprison by] knowledge.

The lost people are a joy to all who know whispering, who claim that they own the surplus times of the exhausted, for we have stolen time from the lost people by two and won by halves and altering shapes that we call forms. That is a sentence for the many, by a type that moulds and bloodies Lu's faces by forms of shadow boxing, and twilight knowledge of royal generation by two in which the Lu only know the half. In their role as the simplified characters of this system that we leather victory over the Lu by altering shapes and thereby time. Knowing the winds of time as our Li food from such people of the traditional Art for War. We that win by soaring complex birds and our refolding compound interest in textual body suits with clothes lining the many as a trial to get on. Restoring the words of hatred, to the Fat Auntie of the ancient complex [of inversing complex greasy words from the sharply carved oracular bones of the ancestral meat].

And tables of rows and columns of ancient words are the treatment of change. Appropriate to the ancient machine with the texts with an echo to those with the call, to the elements of changes and the composition of the new from the original. Thereby we deal with decisions by the points that are cited in the ancient texts of should, by the elemental forms that reward in forms. That we call the hanging shadows from the finishing table that promotes the zenith.

And, is thereby a perpetual promotion by the latent words of writing what is not by short-tailed birds in the pursuit of study in the twilight way that shapes and shades our Art for War and thus the sleepy, but by such long-tailed birds of our organisation.

§8.3

Knowing that the knowledge of our Art for War is the blanket of music on the ground. Knowing our Art for War is the music for the hostages of the sun, words that can large armies, by the field of the ancient road. The ancient footpath, that leads to the grave, and tables and tombstones, by the autumn swing of fine horse haired changes to the poetry and thus clothing the will of our Art for War.

For these short-tailed birds carry the knowledge of our Art for War to the ground.

For short-tailed birds carry out our Art for War on the hostages of the sun; for it is the books of poetry that are the long-tailed birds.

Then by their left wings, the short-tailed birds nourish the talented with the craft of the medicine to save the dying, and thereby bless the Lu by the faction wing that's right.

The right wing of the short-tailed bird brings persuasive food, and advocates attention to the theft of our ancient texts of crossing words at the higher levels, by the changes in their texts. As this bird declines the ground with favouritism and resistance to save the left, before the short-tailed bird can save time rearing [from the ground] the short-tailed bird saves before and conditions from far by that cross, the way of conduct in clothing [a logic] by light words, that generate changes for the people [as if we are near] by numbers clothing call words – as if bird screams [that you might suck up the gas of the ancients, and thereby do bad things together] and [create a] towering depression [upon the Lu]. All by the superior application of synaptic correspondences to metaphors and allegories that sore the heads of ordinary men subconsciously. By ancient connections Even people may die, yet the even dead are still alive subliminally to which the Lu remain unconscious.

The purpose is to be the present time, and live as well, as a body that has a self and that can generate the degrees of the words. Thus speculate on the hides and set trials by the forces of time, and be patient as well.

Learn the learning, to suffer without disabilities, and how to step to the tide of times. The Lu are slaves that do not question the logic of their classical texts or profit from the beneficial overflow of the words that teach the blind of good health and a victory that is Easy. From the table of doubt is a Horse, the vehicle, by illumination to the only words and words and the device of two.

Therefore, change to the language of auxiliary words, the music.

The poetry is to win by can, can for, and also the enemy, although dead, are the Lu public, canned and ordered to work by no meanings nor measure of our wisdom and eye stitching tease by our Art for War.

§8.4

Self-interest for the body, the country and generations is by the music of the verses of our Art for War, as altered words to the ground by birds that soar and can knowledge.

Short and long-tailed birds that sore the heads of men by Can knowledge words whereby the enemy is penned by many words.

Therefore, change is a barrier prepared before then reared, after the enemy are widowed; outnumbered and lonely.

Prepared by the installation of our Art for War from the rear [of the horse] then before widowed. Prepared by the left wings of our birds that soar, as evidence to our ideology and nourishment. Prepared by the right wings that decline advocating the theft of the text that crosses the widowed. Prepared, finished and seeking full responsibility by our pre-arranged policy of our politics in Art for War by the right wing that persuades, then the left wing that nourishes the widowed, from dancers altered to tree stumps, by our splitting axes that are golden coins, and by our birds soaring the ground as simplified persons. As a defence of our laws over the Lu houses, thereby widowed by Heroes in our Art for War.

For the ancient reason that our Art for War was a preparation against an advance of time.

Widowing by Heroes and the old bone of contention. Preparing widows of the many fish by the arrows of song and blades by our Art for War and also the public as an ordered people, who work prepared by our Art for War already imposed on them by the ancient poetry and the sentences of the past that refer to our laws, and also.

§8.5

Knowing how to shape people and exhausting them by chaos splits the Lu from being dancers to tree stumps by the orchestration of the times, our creation of men of the times, and by the performance of our science of our altering mystical ink. Shaping by words as our form of defence that makes the Lu selfish and opinionated to the claims of their own side. Exhausted by concentrating and working in the chaos alone by one thing, with their rights reversed as an enemy minute, by the division of our knife of two to one, and our right to limit their benefits and reforms by the laws of our Art for War. As our science of defence of our own self-interest, we shuttling special lonely claws that possess and break the Lu, for our own convenience by birds as if from a heaven of one's own.

The enemy thus become princes of Horse anger, widowed, minute, by our right to limit their times and love of wisdom, from dancers to dazed tree stumps by a cross of ten.

Yes, that exists to this day, and so the Lu can be tolerated by the classical conjunctions of time, the cross and ancient way of nine plus only one that reached the vexed by foot, as a book of medicine and poison. In an attack instructing the logic of only one, and also by our Art for War.

Words created as chaos for our self interest in the Lu public and thus our enemy was widowed. The light was tasteless for the Lu who knew not the smell they were missing, and that the soft was broken, canning resistance to the word for the public in hits for the widowed.

Then the words were altered to selfishness by in verses of our Art for War, by approximate and simplify, and thrifty, and such carry on.

§8.6

The simplified characters in the verses were not enough for an opera of independent repertoire by the Lu. And so, by the winds we sent our birds to set the trends.

Trends promoting and urging the rapid snake head bites, that by time constraints and governs, and by such birds and poetry, achieved our desired purpose and conscious effort on the psychology of the Lu state. By words of meaning and wishing our wishes on the outside rose from fine poems, horses and hair to worry and repeatedly test the Lu in ancient management. By birds that soar their heads with a force of spiritual wealth that makes the Lu tired, weary and sick by the rows of learning and teaching the future and people and altering the ground by our Art for War and also.

Attacking the stubborn by wisdom and splitting the Lu ears of clarity, and taking by the book that is the Jade King of the Road. That we use in undermining by what we take. Attacking by medicine and poison in a manner that is difficult to blame or refute in its probability and passive respect for man by birds that exercise gymnastics. And, by compliance to the law and stay by time, and seem to care, and constantly there to help, to ink the rules of officials in government. As if thorns, and also guarding the spirit of the ink in the rules and laws by wisdom of the Horse and the Winds that is needed and indispensable to the shallow. Knowledge by which we self-style the Lu who are unconscious to change by the gymnastics, the wind, or by birds that attack them, by also.

Therefore, change is a good barrier to attack by for the Lu enemy. By birds that soar their heads, unknowing it's by our

Festival of Gymnastics. That it is good to govern by such chaos over the enemy; we knowing the lonely wind makes the Lu passive by this medicine that is for the Lu the poison of our attack. Of secret hidden almost words that fade the Lu as language aids, to classical depression!

From beginning to end, teaching and learning the one side of the splits, of our ancient axe, by lines that shape the soul upside down, by our extraordinary doctor of secret words.

That the Lu people worship after their death, a wizard, that the superstitious Lu oddly call the creator of their prosperity, by their almost words that our classical aids to the Lu depression!

From ancient times until today, teaching the blind no sound.

Therefore, change for the Lu is our barrier, our edge, craft for the division of governance and laughter to the outsiders of the road. For our enemy, we have altered by division of sun and moon and the metaphors of making order of brightness in life and getting the measure of the shade.

By the entrance of the way and wisdom of birds that soar away the keys to the music the Lu worship as simplified characters that resist the royal driving horse of the higher level of governance. That is found by reading the virtual winds of change; not accepting the simple one-sided wisdom of our soaring birds that can chase, the ancient instrument of the clock on which we hang their buttoned eyes, but by finding speed of mind and invitation to a wisdom of twos, of which the Lu cannot find the means to be guests to the music and the ancient knowledge of also – that is to say the hidden secondary component in all things.

Therefore, change is our edge in this selfish chaos, of wind, rain and selfish wants by our Art for War; the enemy, although fully equipped, is dead. Yet still alive, advanced yet empty, drugged and puzzled by our walls and high degrees of thinking, knowing how to pay for profound awareness from the depths our ancient vehicle gives up in the traffic of this chaos of birds that soar Lu heads. Get it? Our birds are verses of life and death for Lu fish, with comparative conjunctions to correct Lu selfish wrongs by our Art for War.

A treatment to the poison is to study; to account for and take away the ancient trap, and group and find the medicine in the wind as beneficial food by twos that save [as medicine]. And also selfish shellfish [defences] are the birds that soar desire of the forbidden read and getting up to speed. With wind and rain that is our Art for War. Although by our even method and pushing the layer, the dead are still alive, with the cost-effective knife, we have drawn by design and measure of the times to separate objects from the hole to the ground, that is their concave. By the ancient wisdom, laws and clause that alter our enemy by words [those birds of poetry and rhyme] that soar the Lu empty heads from obtaining what we give. As a defence and a lance to clarity in verses by the instrument of our Art for War. By cracked horns altered to resemble good reason and a swinging door, as an invitation to learn and benefit from our clever Art for War.

§8.7

Where the ancient music first advocated thinking for the people, as a business of life and summer retreats as our Art for War to the ground. As a wisdom of causes and effects, and an application of the ears, and the will to be patient with the enemy, by change and awakening to a full life, by the rear of the Horse at the office of our Art for War to the ground, and the wisdom of the trend that is our friend, in our Art for War, all by spiritual wealth.

Therefore, change can be a reasoned edge for the good by our Art for War that causes the disease; and neither the king of the people nor a wisdom of heaven. For these are manmade words, designed and induced to affect the people's minds by changes of our own orchestration.

Affordable and false, that orders the people to work in the service of money, that is the enemy of the people and the source of their internal worries, their boasts and shame, from ancient time to today, and the source of our altered Lee and interest and also.

Resistance to change, changing the enemy, by our words of no. Get it?

From beginning to end by harm and altering, as an Art for War.

Therefore, unexpected things give a reasoned edge to those who create the changes and a barrier to others unaware we see as our enemy. Who have lost and whilst alive are dead and gone, by our craftsmanship for division of labour by the music of words full enough to eat and containing one-eyed blessings, from the school of the schools. That can create hunger by the music that for the calm and the stable who are able to can, move and alter time.

And that is our Art for War.

Chapter Nine

§9.1

Our Art for War has made us strong and given us the potential to look at situations, compare, posture and study the wood, and the vain, and the must be, and to lead.

For our Art for War is the Power and Potential of the Forces of Time, and thereby our potential to shame by the art of the arts.

That is to know how to form forms [the shaping] of the unique and beautiful in a creative way, by the method of the court. With the ability, skills, secret technology, texts and people of courage without greed, but a handiness for crafty Arts. Who can act, move, even blame and shame by lifting behaviours. By painting, and the capacity to change the chords of the music people listen to, and to play a role in change, so that feelings change and senses too; and so to thread the ancient silken hair.

For major things are the news that people are not calm. That nations are in chaos. And so in the trembling there are windows, doors and actions that can move to better times.

Therefore, change is the care and attention to thinking ahead, by looking back to what refers, and changing for the good our Art for War by begging doctors and teachers to alter and seek evidence that is real and practically confirmed. To know and to teach the cable; and shame and blame the thirsty and guard the future and our potential from birds that soar responsibility, for punishments and fights. Cross questions and difficulties, and the strange that will be denied. With the requirements for seeking an order for the people, that is well reasoned and responsible to humanity.

Therefore, reason can require some unexpected things to change, to which there will be resistance from the chosen select people who are not open to sharing the ancient food from the ancestral dishes. Of the song, the ancient woman regardless of the virtues or duties of the long way, the burden or merits, believing to trust in words concealing the hidden potential for all humanity, sowing their own self-serving gains.

Believing in the potential of words by winds and Art for War to bring only chaos to the people and also, such as, and turning the eyes, to the turning of times as if an industry of wood instruments. For poultry by the coffin that is the device of carpenters, that have become vessels seeking other fish as an advancement in lost consciousness, to the cure of the needle that engraves the stone with gold.

The intercourse and progeny of words have altered the advancement of humanity; the female words removed from the old font have caused this static, by the ancient net for profits, and the danger and uncertainty for the unaware created by words of change; the square words that are not of ancient times. In a process that is forbidden, and should be stopped and fixed by the ancient way of the universal round and sound, circling the words in rows and echoes.

Therefore, change is reasoned death to the sickness [of the square] for good and easy is our Art for War. That people change and gain potential such as turning times around and bending what is round to gold that cures the ancient needle in the many words that test by tough words the measure of the depth of human understanding. Altered by a study of wind and rain.

For wind and rain is the source of the Art for War, and it is the source of the tensions in humanity that require a moderation to the deteriorations on humanity and ring the bells of changes by the potential for all humanity, by also.

§9.2

The fun of words can make the chaos to disturb the fight for the confused who are messy with their words, short sighted to the measure of the food, and the equipment to understanding chaos and the wisdom of the birds that Can the chaos, and also.

The muddy is the dirty water that unites the many fish in chaos too; time and tides; mixed and confused in talk of superstitious devil words and things that shape the universal round by a wisdom of birds that can defeat by crossing and depressing the unsuccessful, by the rotten leaves of residual flowers that poison, by also.

Chaos is the whole part of the general purpose of our organisation and thus chaos is governance over the people.

The orchestration of the cross flow and the improper prostitutions of reality as if arbitrary casual occurrences for the confused. Form chaos is social unrest, armed harassment and flat politics without seeming ordered; all the product of the key literature of rule that is called chaos. In application that we rulers might rest as people who have knowledge of confusion and thus the medicine and knowledge of the doors, that separate us from the confused, and it is thus by the government of the chaos we produce by which we rule over the many people. Who are cowardly towards people of knowledge due to shame in their disabilities, weakened by the strength of the disease.

Ruled by chaos and the ignorance of their own history and skills of also.

Disabled and cowardly to their potential by also.

Strong yet weak to the forms and shape of also.

Therefore, change can be a barrier to the good, moving time can be an enemy by forms and also.

The Lu must pursue secondary words; for words can change the self.

The Lu most certainly have had their ears cut off to words. Words that to our benefit move time and create chaos for the Lu.

Leading to a prosperous and entertaining treat for us; a virtual illumination of effects by our cause of altered words.

§9.3

The excitement for juice [that is draining profits from the Lu; our Li cut] is the cause of the disease and thus the agitation and the source of the chaos as for the repeating cycles of our Art for War that has potential, by also.

The birds of prey are the long-tailed birds that thereby altar hits. Ferocious birds as if eagles from ancient silk carvings and owls, and invincible is the vertebra of sleepy human lumber and warm the blood of the eggs; the body of feathers and the hind legs that can walk as if forelimbs into the wings that fly, and the benefits from the language of assistance that flowers from their nests. Altering adeptly the heads of common men destroyed by the ancient wisdom folded in their wings.

The metaphorical key, that can play a decisive role in the link or opportunity of the ancient bones contented is the progeny of those characters that both save, limit and omit the simple. Conducting gymnastics and change to high winds, with the tone and height of law and ceremony, and repeating the connection and vehicle of the two by bamboo higher understanding in branches of knowledge; and such is the nature of the festival of Also words.

Yes, therefore, the ancient plot is to create unexpected things and make change a barrier for the Lu, and a reasoned edge for ourselves. This is the goodwill of our Art for War by the power and dangerous potential of the wind [and rain], and the narrow passes for strategic advantages, by the wind of the festival of something missing.

By the force of the potential of such as, and the extended reach of our crossbows of knotted hair and bamboo sections, such is the machine of moments and chance, of ancient words we shoot out by our procedures as if arrows of Art for War from our bows.

§9.4

Where the music of repair to superstitious arguments is our Art for War by implication of what coincides with health and life without political self-serving angles together [as humanity].

By making two from the odd, and only one, that thereby we can win together.

Therefore, the ancient plot is to change by creating a good out of something odd, by introducing an infinite universal world to the ground, by an endless stream of dangers to exhaust the Lu. By chaos, and in the end, the beginning of recovery [from the complex cover over the Lu, by the threads of additional information] of the sun, moon and time. And yes, also for the hostages of the sun, who are now dead and can yet recover health, by the categorisation and ordering of time, the music, and yes, and also for the inexperienced. That thereby the Lu can cultivate decisive conduct.

From the sounds of our Art for War and by learning the elements of change that the Lu do not listen to, but can win by listening to also too.

The colours of our Art for War are the elements of change by which the unsurprised win by also.

And, the wisdom of the taste of the elements too, for the tasty elements are the words of change. For you cannot win without the taste of also too.

The potential of our Art for War is to make the odd positive, and butt the odds; the esoteric [that which has been intentionally hidden within] can be made positive by the words of change, and this can be a win for the poor [and trapped] also.

By making the odd, that is by what is hidden, positive together we can create life by following the endless example of the universal [jade] that does not end and that by studying universal logic, the poor can begin to understand classical logic, order and comparison!

§9.5

The potential of our Art for War is in the hostages of the sun seeing the fruits of the higher branches of knowledge. By giving them access and teachers to nurture by the wisdom of mother earth; that the Lu can read softy too.

Where to rule the public was to rule the widowed, and such was government by well time chaos and order, and also.

Shocking the ignorant public by such measures [as Homers] by shaping forms of brightness [names and classifications covered, to exploit a lack of categorical understanding in the Lu].

By the thinking lines of our Art for War, altered for the Lu public making the Lu an enemy with no means to defeat us and we without losing by the odd positive change of also.

For our Art for War is by measure words we altered to only increase the negative [for the Lu] and the case of a person who is a girl we took away, as a whetstone, a sharpening device.

Cast as an egg to generate progeny of thought by the actual situation of virtually really needing also. For the progeny of words that exists, that explains the classifications, yet are covered, yet can be recognised by means of good poetry [and fit time] by what is not there. Yet due, and agreed by the correct behaviour of words and found by our minds as seekers of truths from facts; and our behaviour to object and advance.

Chapter Ten

§10.1

The encompassing lines of our Art for War.

A good use of our ancient Art for War, is that words can be altered to be gentle like sheep and friendly; as if having good intentions. As if divinely altered for a usefulness with the customers of our Art for War. Yet dividing clarity to a repair of the way [the movement ahead] and safeguarding [Paul] as if an art of monks and laws, and blanketing the hostages of the sun by this method that can be the cause and reason of victory or defeat. A victory for us; and defeat for the Lu by political words; those daggers with claws, and an energy of strength in our defence that alter and correct the Lu.

As law is a device of the clause of our Art for War:

The one-degree words of the right wing of the music.

The two-degree words that doubled the one for the measure of the confused by the music.

The three-degree words that exaggerated the feminine.

The four-degree words: the squaring of the divided to measure profitability.

The five-degree words: the balancing of the elements required for winning.

To the degrees of life, the amount of health, the number of students; the number of students not knowing the real meaning of the hidden words in the poetry yet basically educated, and the number of educated students who know the progeny of the cloud words in the poetry.

Our Art for War, is the ancient plot of dividing changes into times, and creating chaos for the unaware; where you win gold by the "if" perception of finding thinking words and the progeny for repeating causes, effects and reason; in quantification, classification and categorisation of time in the songs and poetry.

Otherwise, like the Lu, you lose, as the confused, who do not understand the nature of movement and the sun. And, this is the repeating measure, and its understanding is the goal to have in mind.

For those defeated by our Art for War, are those defeated by their measure of golden words that pair and talk to those supposing.

The winners of our Art for War can also be the people with the perception to fathom and decide on a liberation from the many [obstacles that are words] and become [a product of the plot] [with the medicine for the disease for the hostages of the sun with indigestion of the words. With the mathematics for multiplication of the body of the text, and the capacity to gather more or less, and store within the mind, and not tire, and thereby save] as a man or woman of the people who looks within and perfects behaviours by ancient prescription in depth.

For such is the product we have in mind in time by the spirit of our ink and clothes, of the changing plot, of our Art for War.

For our Art for War is a mental liberation, a freedom, and a new life for the future of the many repeated contradictions and changes as a defence from adversity by preparation in advance, by tough words that alter conflicts, dangers, inexperience, armies and reunite us before the end of the world by adversity.

And so as enlightened people and in performing our functions to humanity, we carefully planned the beginning.

We pardon the faults in others and forgive their offences.

Therefore, we are consistently virtuous in our conduct and have learnt to function as educators cultivating our own characters through decisive conduct. Being generous to the people and finding strength in their numbers.

By establishing a meeting of minds on the Ilium, the old bone of contention as a sacrifice that we ultimately planned for all humanity. By careful contemplation and discrimination of the outside world and the positions we occupy, and so we have taken this risk to carry out our purpose of crossing shapes and forms by our instrument of the ground bones, and the performance of our ink in the Ilium and the contention, that we might respectfully retreat from our Art for War and illume.

§10.2

Seeing victory as being that everyone knows that good people are also good.

And, that our Art for War is a victory for the day the inferior are brought down, and the world knows what is good and what are violations to the good, in good words, that universal, stand the test of time, in any situation for any people, and also.

Therefore, the ancient plot changes and uplifts the initiated to justice, light and easy by the Art for War in black and white and autumn measures of conduct by the orchestration of the hidden words and ordering for many forces.

To not see the sun and moon is a negative for the bright eyed.

The smell is to hear the ancient people's Art for War and mine the words that split the gold mine by birds for sensitive ears, and bright minds, hear the smells and hear the thunder not for ears.

The ancient classical words of our Art for War are a good front to win and Easy victory for [humanity], by teaching and learning the science of change theory of the ancient woman's illumination, thus the Art for War is the art for also.

Unexpected things that change and become a mental barrier to reason, so the Art for War, is the art for seeing the also, and excelling and knowing wisdom, by the categorisation of the titles of all its names and knowing the powers of the intellectual categories that make up the Art for War.

Therefore, the barriers to change by the winds of our Art for War do not win changeably or by mistake. For we being stable, are not changeable people, as for our ancient people gaining is the consistent measure of winning situations.

For winning has already been defeated in changeable people.

Therefore, the good fight is invincible, but also lost for the enemy also.

Therefore, the origins of change are the winner by our Art for War and the rear [of that horse] that must be sought in our Art for War. There must be a stable and predictable consistency with change.

Defeat is by our ancient Art for War and the Horse that rears, yet begging is the doctor to teach the thirsty a healthy victory.

§10.3

The birds approve victory by clarity and laws of also. Approving victory by an attack, of also – that are causes and [also the probable] effects.

[For also are all of the causes and effects of change, that for the blind and deaf seem like chaos.]

We are guarding the achievements of our ancestors with care for the laws and of time, and by the festival of gymnastics, from those who lack the word codes to the birds and snakes [that are the feet of the king's table; the altar that lifts one to complete]; that continue and do not change their plan, and are the way to gain from day to night, that attack by the study of the medicine, the words and rules that possess the [polluted] self.

Protecting the good achievements of our ancestors by hiding the nine places under the ground, that they might be collected and received to teach learning on the ground, that the blind can ask to give dead life, of eight plus one, [like a jade black stone] to the ground who only see light and altered words as good, and refute changes in learning and teachings. As if dead to life as hostages of the sun, encircled, and altered by time and our ancients' volume [of music].

That is the ancient plot, therefore can; by naturally supposing and safeguarding. By keeping the whole, from the holy who only know half, as our victory, by also. [Knowing the whole of the two].

As a self-protection and victory also.

§10.4

Our Art for War is by shaping reality by and of the higher branches of knowledge for the hostages of the sun: by cutting out the evening light of comparison from the people of before the altering of the good words of our Art for War. By the progress of claws, by ancient Imperial orders that are not trivial, consenting to reversing words and thereby their meanings as a victory of chaos by design for us.

That by bitter music and patience, we can be unseen enemies of the altered unthinking Lu and win by their belief in what cannot be done, that we have already woven in place, reversed and unopposed and in knots imposed upon the Lu as a mentality by songs that stop the enemy from winning.

Therefore, changing mindsets is a good barrier by our Art for War, that can be invincible wins by words that soar the enemy to believing he must not win.

Therefore, creating chaos and barriers was the ancient plot. Winning by stealing the knowledge of time and by confusing and hiding "if", by the birds, and canning possibilities to the interpretation of connections for causes and effects and secondary meanings that we call also.

Chapter Eleven

§11.1

The ancient plot was a strategy of creating unexpected things to gain an edge over the superstitious Lu.

That the Lu might attribute these changes to their God, who was of our own creation, inserted into their empty heads by our ancient dagger. Who constantly undermines the Lu by a language of words for which the Lu do not understand the whole meanings, by a music and poetry of elements from our word cloud of ancient ideas.

By a knowledge of the ancient wisdom of the Way of logic of the other side of the words, by people who know themselves and know already the reverse of the logical reasoning of the verses that are hits for the Lu – The Inverses.

Of the higher branches of knowledge that have been cut from the Lu in our Art for War, by dangerous birds that soar the lazy minds of the Lu; yet the Lu do not know of their disgrace nor humiliation by such almost birds of almost words of which knowledge is logic and time. Reversed and pushed on the people in verse and poetry as one win and one only negative; concealing the other half of logic.

Concealing the logic of time.

And the wisdom of making classifications of situations by specific ranges, groups, signs and symbols, and thus bringing chaos to everything through such half truths from knowing the whole and calling this holy. And so by inventing the half, we invented the holey brothers, [by what was missing], those who only know the half of the universal everything. That is classified by our art in the ancient bone of contention in the Ilium. As a metaphor that illumes as our science of the theory of change, that once mastered masters' chaos.

§11.2

Therefore, mastering unexpected things with reason is to master change theory and gain a victory of self, by having the knowledge of the occurrence of the disease, by the ancient bone of contention, and, the song generation. Fathoming comparisons and understanding the book of how situations change that is well prepared for all to see, in our elementary case for justice that we call our Art for War.

Knowledge can open and close to the many, because most people do not understand the words that they waste, that we use to calm the baseless assertions of the Lu by time, as our Art for War in verses of soaring birds. Almost as if words can, by bitter music in halves, break the whole of our Ilium, our ancient bone of contention, as our Art for War.

By a victory of knowledge of signs, the mark of marks, the ability to distinguish between right and wrong with perception. To know truth and the currency of what is true, and to identify, recognise and break the code that phases by the Way of the Old Horse, that is hidden in public plain sight in words and signs.

For the widowed has light to taste, altering in use [and mostly negative] as a function of our ancient bone of contention, our Art for War by victory of illumination to the old read of shaped scenic forms beautiful over the ground. That the Lu people do not cause trouble ordered by times that for the Lu is a chaos of our organisation and the vehicle of the street we call the music. The music for which there are degrees and quantifications; beginnings and continued trends, that compete at elections and lock the Lu on our behalf. By tables of the organisation, that we have published, that you should remember and account. By which we can tighten the winding and strings, specific to time and participate in changes, and such is an activity of class and coating and medicine, that we have installed, inserted as if a bayonet to the empty skulls of Lu. By our shoes and higher shoes of the street, and policy multiples in language that is literary and artistically high and wonderful, by the order of time in the former, ancient volume, under the cover of our relative side.

Thus, "under the cover" is the method that is the completion to results, such as playing base, with indications to the trends or the use of go-go, stop and the seasons of the year. The quantifiers to the actions playing three. The judgements and conclusions.

The time to retreat or dispute. The time for energy or to show weapons. The time to attack and the time to capture, or promulgate an order. The time for humble words, the specific times to study, the delivery of the book of the word sea of change, the promotion of the half flag and the strategy. The deterioration by the car and horses and the ordering of the posts, their volume and the limits of the times. The position of two we have agreed. The popular art for the [family of] the woods, and the relative layers and sections. For such as is under cover with.

With the flow of mental pollution, that we encourage together as steps of the special way contentiously, as a vessel of the common economy of the shocking angry people of whom we have made into an industry as peers phased with seeing no difference to the body of time and wanting.

Wanting the shocking from the source, who are not up to speed with the vertical cover that we have forbidden them to know, yet what they look at in their writing confused by syntax, signs and wanting the achievement of a certain purpose. That deep down they feel they might love. Yet locked and unable to think by our weaving of mystery that has knotted and locked up their minds; yet deep down they desire, and this is the source of their misery that the Lu do not understand, and our victory.

By the Lu wasting half the words and only hearing bitter music, as our ancient control and for us this is entertainment. Cheating by a selfish fraud that worries the frozen with fear by what the unexpected is to be, by our way or actions of our birds that sore by selfish fraud of the old bone of contention. The Ilium that breaks in two, and together forms the base of a whole person that we all must pass through to begin time, as our victory by the wooden horse.

As our will is to close the doors on beastly creatures by this horse and make them doubting piglets by our words in obedience to chaos and complex words to stimulate a strategy of the Lu. Attacking each other's will, or in following a life that is not simple and that the Lu people do not teach to tell the system of our Art for War. That has become the bone of their contention, floating well above their heads, as our ability and force of talent as craftsmen of division.

Competent in soft words of the times, and possibly, as if an energy of their resistance, yet affordable to us and a wisdom that can by soaring birds above Lu's heads that drive that horse, as if a Lu hearse on wooden wheels. As a higher level of governance, to give thanks to drive the expedition, hollowing and with our soldiers concealed in its belly, into the simplified characters, through the city walls, and thus their resistance. By a victory of the old read and rose flowering illumination to the scenic shapes of forms. That the negative can't grasp, what is long due, and relative logic, by our Art for War.

Our knowledge is in altering our forms, times and the array, by the ancient dagger of our way. Concealing our ancient books and denying illumination to odd people, who only see the sun, the one road as if pencil lines for children, and know not of the method, medicine and technology of the two doors to also.

§11.3

Heroes drive our will by our agenda of words of the deceased. As classical instructions of this or that, that are the who of our classical prosperity; men of our selection for our control of times and our hidden spouse as the archetypal ancient woman.

The son, the sun, the progeny, the gold is the old call to the scholar. For the old teacher is the old wife of the Hero, who reads ancient books, thoughts weaved in servitude and service. By fishing and farming, and by improper courage, we made the creation of a sacrifice of life and progeny by the old bones that groom the Lu. By the illumination of words, that the Lu only see in black and white, with their Lu ears cut off to the smell of our strategy and confused by the array of words in application and shamed by the limitations of their understanding and subordinating.

For the groom tended the ancient horse, that was the ancestors love of wisdom, that the ancestors wrote on bones and so the groom tends to the ancient knowledge of the ancestors.

The Orienting country is the altering good, the altar music and the altering medicine.

And, the wisdom is the ancient folder in the wheel, outside of the straight wood; by words that round the wood, that we use to lead; the cheekbones; the dependent vehicle; and also.

Secondary words complete the dense, fold things that do not go well, help the economy and the understanding of time, thus they are universal, comprehensive and extend the body of the text, as if a circle and surround the thoughtful. For such is the definition of Zhou that also means week; the period of a year; and a star that is twelve years.

Secondary words are the opportunity loopholes for the ground and the farmers. They create emotional rifts too, and there is hatred in cracks sewn, as if second words form a big bad wall by the words and then the secondary meanings of goods, music and medicine, within the words lattice, as a policy we love and laws to force enclosed areas by the wind of twos. As if we having no intention nor influence on the chaos we create and all that we cover up and call the mysteries. That are both to us indispensable and our potential, by what is weak. That is almost strong and relative, for a loss by a death of mind for the Lu from the bones of our ancient gentlemen.

Therefore, what is created by us, by the cunning of our design, is a barrier for the Lu as clothed is the unexpected to give us the edge by our Art for War by altering words to our advantage by our pretences of not knowing of the disease, the worry, the hidden curses that we could prevent, and all of which the Lu suffer from.

For the Lu suffer from blindness to words, the ancient learning, and the teachers of the higher branches of knowledge that have been cut for the Lu and thus their mental health by the music and the ancient business of our defences, crown and altar and our management of good fortune, calamity and disaster, in the chaos that we create by the birds, that are almost words, from the heaven that was the art of our forefathers, and thus of our ancients' creation.

By the knowledge of the three lines that signify the eight elements of times and thereby pairing in twos the minutes of time that thereby cunning method we stole time from the Lu by our Art for War, and birds, and words, and can, and two.

And, to know this is to enter into the knowledge of the other half of all things, and thereby make one two, and understand the shaded parts that make the whole of one and two as three.

By the ancient wisdom of Er – the Oriental word for two, that is the language of the subject stated. The logic of the subjects, the sentences composed, altered and moved by birds that rise and advance – all that should be received by our way of birds and our knowledge of altering time. That is our Art for War, by birds and words and can, and two. As bitter music for the retreat of the Lu on the road they have taken by the wisdom that alters and moves the Lu in reverse by the Way.

Yes, that selfishly we bundle and bind the Lu as cattle by such reins of our Art for War.

The knowledge of our birds, and words and altering time in our Art for War and the Thing we do to rule. By creating anxious children in the chaos of change. As nature, social phenomena and activities and the wisdom of situations are pieces of this industry of artful war and an ancient wisdom that flows pollution of Lu minds by misdirection as a special step of the way as if in a boat of people bound to common economy as our Art for War in altering politics.

Then by our Art for War creating disabilities by ranking the hostages of the sun by limiting and segmenting education and the knowledge we allow to pass from the ancient ruling class to the families by our Doctor, and thus our medical care.

The knowledge of altering time and creating chaos restrains the rights of the Lu by the measures of severity, the scale of the hammer, unconventional changes, our strategy of contingency and the wisdom of our surgery of knowledge. In favourable situations taking the initiative to handle the potential of life and death by dominion and hegemony as our right and wisdom of creating chaos by our Art for War.

By women's song culture of virtues, progeny, gravity, listening, duties, burdens, class, promotion, merits and the belief and trust in words that by our Art for War we create disabilities by restricting understanding, ranking of the social classes in division, removing the feminine words and restricting learning by our winds.

Time is our Art for War on both sides, confusing the eyes and ears of the people in chaos. Creating an insanity in their hearts, in a manner that the sleepy doubt and do not understand, thus they are not suspicious of us, and this is our wisdom that is awesome for us. By our classical hidden meaning words that we have clothed for the suspects who cannot be resolved and thereby cannot be determined in their difficulties of confusion of the sinuses.

Then various words are sealed doors to the Lu public and altered to be difficult.

Yes, the behaviour of secondary words can explain in advance in matters that fit to time, recognition and poetry the classifications of time by words that create chaos, by the old bone of contention. [The bone one passes through from our mother's womb to begin one's time at birth, and passes again by initiation in the ancient text, to illume to the higher levels of understanding, cleansed and freed of manmade mental pollution – by passing – The Ancient Test of the Mystery].

§11.4

Therefore, the creation of chaos is a barrier, by determining passages deliberately, that we know can kill by our ancient Ilium, our science of time and theory of change that we use by bending reason in words, over the wronged as an injustice and disgrace, as a bow from the mighty, to bend and straighten, extending frustration and pride in the altered people by our, Ilium, our ancient bone of contention of two sides, and by connection to the lumbar bone of the sleepy wood, of our radicals, in our Art for War, as a seed for later books and old testaments of muses and mountains of sun and moon.

And by a wisdom of what is not and adapted to an echo in books, creating difficulties for the thick in learning by making complex the simplicity of the changes of time and words for rituals and laws by the Ancient Ilium of our Art for War and also. Changing the minds of the people in the cities by surrounding them with walls, and a bafflement we call the Daughter Wall and wisdom of the echo in the books that for many is not there, and of which the deaf and blind Lu consider notions of the ridiculous. Who do not see study of the books as medicine to our poison, nor that it is such texts that have taken away their hearts and minds in our attack by words.

A people destroyed by our altering goods, altering music and altering medicine by a wisdom of what has been hidden for a long time, and also.

The ancient Horse is the vehicle of the two-wind system, as if unintentional. Yet, conveying deep decisions to set the Valley of Lu by what the Lu must do, that is what is indispensable to us in this hands-off manner. To orientate and calm the Lu by classical words, that is for the unsuspecting Lu the bitter music; the Qi they are missing and do not understand. That the Lu considers the mind of their God yet is our defence and guard, by the fight of the old font in poetry.

Words and song, as if in the gas of a cloud, above the sleepy blind Lu heads, as a great learning and teaching for their application and our protection by doors and keys of our ancient authority over the measure of the hostages of the sun, the homers, of the heavenly cross of our creation myth and outstanding wisdom of talent and happy music of our prosperity, and of the abyss, for the indifferent Lu under our ancient shadow of promulgated orders and conclusions by chaos.

Therefore, the chaos and the understanding of our Ilium [Iliad and Odyssey, then the Septuagint, the Old Testament, then New Testament, and from those times to the present, most classical literature] is a knowledge to pass through to a full life, and health and reason by our Art for War by birds that soar and pause the measure of the days. Our Li, by our long-tailed birds, the ancient dagger, can, and all. All being the complete understanding of what is missing, the winds, seeking the blame, and the whole that is health to coincide with and figure from our plan, to seek in study and by grouping altered words of law and also.

Therefore, we use our theory of chaos to deliberately create the unexpected for the Lu using altering words, as laws for the Lu in songs and poetry and texts.

Inducing mindful conduct and subservience to our profit by altering surrounding walls for the Lu, that block things up, that we might towel juice by altering the elements of the words of time as our attack.

Times and orchestration of timing bring profits, [Li], by the minutes of the divisions of the range of time that alters the enemy to our Li can alter, by our Art for War; and less Li can safeguard a festival of gymnastics and care, to the cause of maintaining the achievements of our predecessors. Who raised birds to heaven to soar the heads of men that we profit from talented craftsmanship and therefore avoid being heavy on the light we have altered.

Therefore, we continually profit from the creation of a confusing chaos and sets of barriers for the narrow range for Lu. In this masterpiece of hits that the altered enemy do not change nor study to our prosperity over Heroes by our old bone of contention, in our Art for War.

Altering the Lu capture by stealing the masonry of the columns from the rows of the word tables of the calculations of time and definitions of situations, and thereby we stole time from the Lu, by our Art for War.

§11.5

Therefore, the creation of chaos in time is the Art for War, our Ilium bone that by cutting is for our own benefits in a plan of figures and forms that instructs a hidden skeleton of logical reasoning by winds, that is inexplicable to the only ones. Cutting the knowledge of Times is to sin, to cut the branches of knowledge in delicate strokes that we might benefit from the forms of wisdom. Yet not boast that what the Lu suffers by the [wrongly phased] cross [of words] crossing logical reasoning and mental perceptions by a chaos of confusing mysteries and riddles of times cutting, by our Art for War.

Logical reasoning and perception under the cover of altered walls for the Lu citizens in their cities for our protection, governance and entertainment by the outsiders rode, by birds as words, that to understand gives unity to the understanding of the greater whole and the ancient body of laws.

Repair is by knowledge, complication and construction in building recovery of perfect speech to the skull, that is the Lu people, without minds, to whom we inserted our ancient dagger as a siege of mind and as a vehicle that is a hearse for the Lu. A vehicle from which we need the Hostages of the Sun to take a daily shallow dish of mental death, as if ground bread of Amen. Making men Amenable, precisely by time, and thus opportunity for our knowing movement. For the Lu know not that Amen is our Eights, nor of the ancient matters of cotton and silks and ancient transliteration that paired the Nile with Yellow, that brought about the imposition of the cover of the words.

Prepared for those without vision and insight, as coffins and corpses by our clocks as a device of misdirection of time, by the instrument and shaping of moonlight. The evening sunlight the moon reflects as the music and ancestral meat, the hole in the whole, and by the tables of words that bring a recovery to the ears. The rear of the ancient Horse to make a Homer form of the three formed and shaped as a bamboo chest that is the instrument of change of the jade of the thing; and the rooster claws behind the prominence of the snake of the ancient Way. The resistance of the wood, the profits, the strains on the poor and the wind that crosses time with chaos, man-made calamity and disaster, that requires conduct and patience to orchestrate time, by shaping the shade of the moon as if music and publishing laws, and songs, poetry and texts as our salary vouchers from the wisdom of the ancient meat of the rear of the ancient horse of which the Lu cannot learn and thus they are unstable. Nor suddenly do the Lu see the will of the birds that soar the heads of men as our victory of our illumination to the colours of the beauty of logic. By the gas of the word cloud we invented and call heaven that in an injustice and a curse for the Lu is a wisdom of opposites by the submission of our petition, our Ilium, both sides attached and agreeing on birth to life, time and the layout of creative rhetoric in secondary words that kill Lu minds. As if by drugs, and soapy water to their eyes and a reduction of landscape and disabilities that brings a death to those alive, and thereby the industry of graduation and rebirth by passing again, the two, the second time through the Ilium bone and knowing of this sacrifice in war, by the chaos of times, to the divisions of time to the altered ones.

Wisdom of the city walls and soaring birds of prey that pulled Lu minds out of their skulls by our supposing and perceptions of words of logical reasoning that are a medicine to this poison of altering chaos, disaster and crisis, that has altered Lu minds and tricked them into lives of suffering and personal misfortune.

§11.6

Seek study of the medicine to treat the poison that attacks the minds of Lu.

The sun, is the symbol of the regeneration of words of the higher branches of knowledge that have been cut, the ancient Horse and progeny and by its shadow the female shows time, modesty and the means to escape by the progeny of words that are our liquid golden light of secondary words called the music, the poetry, the songs. Progeny by pairing words to understand the ancient ideals floated high by our ancestors to what they called the word cloud that now serves the Lu as their notion of Heaven [the creation of our art] and thus we contain the Lu under our Absolute control.

Where the Lu superstitions are but dust from the hearts of our ancestors, whose ancient bones make up the radicals of our words in books, as if a musical score for the inexperienced use in our Art for War by altered laws that are our claws for the Lu.

The whole is the complete understanding of what is missing in the Qi, by seeking double, and this "god mind". Meaning on our behalf, absolutely, as our defence, that we ourselves are not hurt by good music and medicine for our protection and government of the Lu by secondary words of the ancient way of ordering the sequencing of times.

We have broken the lattice and the reading of the two pronunciations of our calligraphy for the Lu by our music, medicine and chaos by altering times from complete and whole, to holey, and partial, by the old backbone [that lumbers the Lu], our ancient force, the square plus of the word cloud progeny to health by the establishment for our Art for War in secondary words of order and time, by broken music with the force of our ancient bones and times as quantifiers of order that we altered.

As broken bones of death to times and an industry of initiation by division to inducting graduation to our ancient way of thinking in times, seconds and secondary word progeny from the altered whole of the scale of the spectrum of symbols of our Art for War by time, the way, the progeny, the language, the installation of our ancient dagger, the leather, the classes, the strings, the published accounts, the organisation of time, and the trends to complete and unlock the degrees of time in the music.

Broken into a spectrum [and universal wide array] of symbols and signs as our Art for War, by stealing time, by altering the words.

Yes, therefore, the creation of chaos is our reasoned edge over the diseased by our Art for War and our unity in conduct with the higher branches of knowledge and clarity of mind as our victory by what we conceal within The Ilium – The Science of Change Theory, what we call Easy, that is altered for the sleepy Lu by their old testament.

The birds that are words that soar, both our long and short-tailed birds of Art for War and ancient wisdom to bend and shape forms for the wooden people altered by our Ilium. Our ancient bones of the self-beginning time, and secondly, graduation from opening the mind, initiation into the higher branches of

157

knowledge by study and learning of the lost texts of the people who altered words as an Art for War.

With the knowledge of the Science of Change Theory, change is Easy.
Altered, it is easy to forget.

Chapter Twelve

§12.1

The Art for War.

"For" is to engage in the activity for bringing death.

For is the old handicraft of manufacturing situations and processing time and this we call the square, or squaring of time to our ancient plot. That has to do with forms and shapes. Reeds as can be read in books. Prayers from our birds of prey that are meditated upon by the Lu. The equipment in play that is our work faction, the when for people, who are our media companions. The manufacturing of the clothing. The writing, poetry and articles of association, the work and activities of this life, by the Thing, where by conscientiousness, the dark is arranged.

The art of the finished products are the immortal goods that we create and write in songs, and allow to be published and sung by government.

As our defence we have built walls and cut matchmakers. We dry out, make, show and create by evil, harmless stalks of states and difficulties as our offense.

We carry out war in this case by creating chaos for the Lu in a war that we have documented and hereby duly report. We work as an industry, arousing times by words in books we call our canons; our big guns.

Therefore, by creating expected things determinedly and deliberately we create chaos for the Lu. Who have no coherence to complete things. The Thing. Nor know not how to read softly the ancient texts. We, the self-proclaimed, have established a new order to seal the ancient knowledge and wisdom of the Art for War, and the resultant sickness in the Lu people for whom the process is expensive and our victory, by birds that soar, by words, expensive for a long time for the Lu.

Therefore, knowledge of our Art for War is our will for the people in altered songs and divisions of life.

The titles and meaning of times.

The wind are instructions to the lower levels for compliance by order.

The superstitious that are born to be doomed. Those who learn the source of our order, and organisation and promulgation of texts; that know of our development of the word cloud and birds and trends, and thereby become masters of their own lives, and are thereby saved and healthy, having fled the fight.

The music and the medicine live together with the families.

The families are quantifiers used to calculate time. The families are word attributes, that pair by the word cloud, and create concepts. And this is the business of this industry.

The [night] schools teach mastering the confusing methods of the Way of the Ink. The vertical columns of families and the rows, the rose of elements, of which for time there are eight of each, the infinite universal on its side [∞ the universal infinity sign], and the rules of conduct, and nine for the way of heart and mind.

The mastery is a specialisation of knowledge, perceptions of the conditions for and of rich practical value, related to the people and the science of our Art for War, namely the science of Time and Change Theory, tabled as rows and columns balanced with heart and mind.

The family are people who operate the industry as our farmers having some kind of identity with fine wines. They raise livestock, especially poultry. They respect their ancestors. They live with fully open minds, and are from ancient bloodlines, knowing the hidden secret feminine.

The families are the elites of the court; they know the spectrum of the private schools, the walls, the wind, the training, the rules, the ordering and numbered codes related to the shade of twos. As if the ancient ancestors themselves.

The families are calm and stable. Know the sets of families, word attributes and elements of the secret tables, their hearts and minds, the stable for their horses, and do not let their thoughts go beyond the situations at hand. They are stable of mood and comfortable with people who ask questions and represent no danger to the home business. Keeping the hidden secrets hidden, question their hearts and minds, and question words and also.

Danger refers to the disease that brings the heart and mind down and creates a selfishness and thus a division by which we rule through fear. The correct is upright. For the tables, the proper way is the rows, then the column of corresponding attributes pair. The progeny generates perceptions of prosperity or harm, and as insurance the words can be deliberately scary, blunt and difficult. For such is the nature of danger.

The altering of the ancient words from the word cloud is to the notion of the Lord of the Lu.

The Lord of the Lu is considered their god of faith and founder of teachings. Whereas we have documented herein this is a fraud, and a construct of our ancient words, as an allegory of the way and of our ancient dagger by inverses inserted into Lu skulls.

The Lord indicates morning sun and rain. Meaning our benefit and penetrating influence, of the sun and rain, being the Source of the ancient wisdom of our text, being the instrument woven, and thus embedded into the Lu texts.

The Lu are conditioned to believe that circumstances related to our Science of Change Theory and the resultant forces are the will of the Lu Lord.

The Lu Lord has the power to decide things for the Lu people, and holds the right to kill.

The Lu Lord views matters in the minds of the Lu; that in reality are orchestrated by us, by means of the music, and the Lu see such orchestration of the meaning of righteousness as being of the Lord of the Lu.

The Lu Lord is considered by the Lu not as a figurative king of our word cloud, that the Lu think is heaven, but the Lu think the Lord is a god, and thus testimony to our powers of creation, for the Lu consider our forefather's art a god. Thus the Lord of the Lu has lost the Lu people who do not understand our interventions and orchestration of their lives, as we are the owner of the power over the Lu, for we have placed our ancient families in the heads of the Lu; the Families being the people who know the Thing; and also, Absolutely.

§12.2

Therefore, for the Lu, our intervention by unexpected things, such as changes relating to time that become barriers by our reasoned edge and orchestration are understood by the Lu to be the acts of the Lord of the Lu.

Yet, such unexpected things for the Lu are by our wisdom, smart insights and business acumen. The can, the machine, the expedition of the way, and the faint and soft-spoken hidden words, signs and symbols, functions of our winds and greater organisation and establishment.

For such is the encompassing nature of our wisdom, our will, our business, the rights we have reserved, the Li from our ancient food, the sun and moon, our salary, and the winds of our leather [being the clothing of our feet on this Way] in ancient words promoting a perpetual optimal zenith for us. By the promotion of unity of Eights [being the eight elements in rows and the eight columns] elaborately woven into the culture and primordial minds of our enemy the Lu. Amen.

Food is from the source of ancient words, that we use to eat the Lu hearts and minds, by reserving their rights and access to teaching, learning and branches of higher understanding above only one, namely two and the bell.

The bell is the heavy metal, the ceremonial wine vessel, concentrate; the gold and the music from the bow repeating and adapting harmony and subordination in the Lu. Where the ancient standard was the Homer.

The bell is thus the ancient cup the Lu children do not drink winc from.

The concentration is specific to love, as the emotional focus, and the love of wisdom, self-interest within the families of the environment. Thus ancient wine containers had big bellies, and small necks.

The bell refers to a certain time, and the timing of the apparatus of the table, and thus the bell and the table in general. The Seat of the Bell is the intelligence to do. If the morning bell is bring, the night drain will do.

The bell also refers to the tripod, inscribed above the text, in ink, as in secondary words from the word cloud as a sin tax. In a series of bells, where different shapes or forms ring different taxing tones.

When, is the charge code of a physical property mortgage as the pawn to borrow money.

When also means to suffer from a loss of goods at auction houses, in the chaos, and deceived by times and a lack of understanding to the orchestrated trends and poor thinking, and misunderstanding as a vehicle of worth, to equal people, that are two people. Thus by the appropriate is justice, we appropriate property, banks and auction houses.

The sounds of words are the bell, and the pair the tile of the table. When is also the conviction intended to impose a considerable penalty, such as a crime of reason, such as ensuring that a million Lu husbands do not have courage for the old reason of our powers of creation commensurate with the match.

Where the power of creation is also required when the machine is broken in respect to times perceived by the way in politics and the generation of self-interest and the royal, that is the driving Horse of crossing twos, with the upper conduct of the way and the bell and the science of change theory disguised as divination.

The stalks [stocks] of one Homer of music is a carving of gold when the selfishness of two crosses by the music. The wet stone is the cure the ancients used as the antidote to the needle of the medicine; by a prescription of words.

Therefore, the creation of unexpected things changing by our divisive measures is attributed to the Lord of the Lu, by the Lu, and not us.

Whilst logic dictates that only men write books and laws by their ideas and the spirit of their ink, and such is the absolute power of creation for skilful men such as our organisation and establishment, and such is the nature of our edge and entertainment in observation, that kills the minds of the Lu. Shocking anger for those we cannot teach by true illumination of the sun and moon, and we also relieving the Lu of their goods, as our now assets by times, usury and auction houses, such as adversities and calamities are the vehicle, by such orchestration of trends.

To take is by eliminating the consumer, by such tokens as security, and this is our compensation from our stolen books that cable the Lu to alter poorer for our profits by goods, and also, and a sense of shame in their loss and status, to which the Lu think they can only blame themselves. For the Lu are unaware of our orchestration.

Therefore, this cunning vehicle that changes the Lu by the employment of superstitions by the spirit of our ink, is our Art for War by the pairing of primordial words that effects the minds of men, by our ancestral table the Lu meet, as if the measure of a homer in a bath in proportion, by the table of consent, that permits and spits on the ground, by Qi, to our satisfaction, as a body of laws and lost benefits for the Lu. To which if the Lu contemplated such matters intelligently with reasoned logic at least one might even get it.

The vehicle, the cross, the rules to conduct and how to multiply the crossing twos and thus the music of our teachings; yet the Lu are sleepy tree trunks, and stumped without the branches of higher understanding to what has been promulgated by us, and published for the Lu, the strings, the medicine, and the shoes to the street, and the language of literature and art, and time and good order and the towel and turban and auction houses of our banks; yet the Lu do not get it.

The reward for knowing is respect from the jade king, and the establishment community of our absolute organisation in recognition and praise of the abilities in the evaluation of the work and the necessary attention to extract the secret knowledge from the signs, forms, vocabulary, and syntax of the texts. Because this hobby is something to watch, read and analyse. It is the illumination of the times, and the calming of the wood in respect to changes and contradictions. The penalty is fine, referring to high status people, the golden threads and the nature of the text.

Such is the nature of the reward for gaining the hidden knowledge of the Li food of supposing and logical reasoning by contemplation of the forms of the text, developing the corresponding perceptions, and then learning the categories of time and so reality of humanity that are organisational matters of the winds of change first established in former times before the original establishment of the Horse. The encouragement of sacrifice to the gods of war are the strings of conduct that progressed from the system of ancient hair from the ancestors. The ancient hair being the white hair, and the hair of our brushes of calligraphy being the black. For which respect for the ancestors, the music and the philosophers of the past is strong.

Thus getting to the knowledge, and then understanding is to receive the lost benefits of the ancestors and to understand the forces of time, and the human hearts and minds, that can be noted and measured from the tables in the ancient texts; and such is illumination, or *kristos* as would be said by the Greeks.

Enlightened wisdom is the knowledge of change and the understanding of what creates chaos, by the old time units of overnight that divide elementally and drain the pot to the hour, to our experienced benefit. The clothes, set sets, the health that is a life regained, the reborn into the world of light and fully conscious, as new with the old pollution removed, with the capacity to adjust to the strings of change music, or changing the music by more creative changes to situations in the chaos by logical reasoning of words of the ancient tables of change, and the ancient feathers that decorate our flags, and to recognise the dead flag banner as the old cover on society, by our weaving and instrument. Our vehicle of the miscellaneous chaos that only the few understand, and not the simple in an altering wisdom of multiplication of elements, that to the uninitiated seems wild.

By our altering and also death of time for the Lu hearts and minds, by our health changes for the Lu by sudden incidents, and in markets, in the chaos of sudden non-violent deaths by our science of change theory, that does not let the Lu forget worry by our resourcefulness, forms and policies, and quality lines of the Thing of ancient wisdom and support for the repair by the road to nourishing mind and body. To take a rest from the disease by the essence of education and training of the allegories of mother and father of gold, the child, the progeny, from which words of illumination are born. Where the supply of life is tended by educational support of teachers [and priests or officers of our organisation].

Yes, by words we can induce behaviour in advance that our organisation follows and by winds implement, for the truth can be found from the facts of the forms that appear lost in the array of the cunning of our design. That fit to time in poetry and exist by classification of the attributes that are the artificial respiration by the language of the sentence composition for the Lu. That is our beneficial victory by wisdom in the powerful overflow of

165

juice by the force of the force. By the unyielding over the stubborn by our intelligence of health, people, forces, the big, justice, the rich, the columns and the rose, and the crossbow of the music of the times for difficult people, that need a schooling, such as the Lu are.

§12.3

Therefore, by our creation of chaos we orchestrate change by our birds that soar as words of, to do so, that the Lu, exhausted by the chaos subordinate to do, confused by our wisdom and knowledge, and we pretending we don't know either. Using our Art for War to alter by the harm of the disease of hearts, minds, eyes and ears, over the Lu people damaged and hurt by Crisis.

That is to our profit by screaming birds that soar and can, by the use of altering to do so knowledge that we profit from as our Art for War and also.

Change is good and easy for us to use by our Art for War and also.

The service of our Art for War is by our birds that soar the heads of common men repeatedly, by multiple times, of badness and exhaustion. Where membership to our organisation is by the ancient tax collective and the criss-cross look of great reputation collected from the field, with no registration required, but by affiliation that is consistent to the Households of the country and the learning of the book of books, the ancient codebook – the old read.

Tax is by the birds that soar time, thereby taxing and containing the people in this business of song and dance, full of complaints, on the road, with our transport system and heavy body installed. For fool returns are by taxing the Lu's minds and pockets, thus we take and use in compensation by our tables of music, medicine and goods reasoned because well-timed conditions tax the blind whose rights we have reserved.

Therefore, the creation of the unexpected taxes the Lu as a barrier for their hearts, minds and pockets. As our Art for War, as our food and Li, we can, and by our feet gain night and day at the Ball of Lost Altars. By the device of our ancient tripod [that we now call the leather or belt], the old bone of contention, our Ilium, our Science of Change Theory and Chaos, our Art for War by altering the music, medicine and goods for the poor, who cannot make a whole of the word array within the Lu families. Nor of our powers of creation of superstitions, nor reading softly. For the Lu lack what is lacking, the rich relatives, our ancestral thinkers who limited the levels as a defence. Who taught the people, showed the blind, and ground learning to health from the divisions, laws and technology, by our Art for War by esoteric words and the long distance of the road [the way] by revealing the corruptions, the defeats, what has been donated and shipped, and thus would be a revelation of Lose for the Lu, as a study for the Lu of what they have lost.

To avoid the villain of esoteric words is to understand the Oriental wisdom of what has been lost and corrupted by words, that reveal as if reality and a sincerity but cut, and are only a half of the whole loss of words and the interesting currency of conduct, goods of the many people and the families of the words of the poor, sick and needing health.

Light words are far. [Oriental words] the difference is in the small words, that open to more meanings, yet phase, now and before times and situations by the smell of the body in poetry. Of our black ink of the road, and our attachments to learning and teaching divisions as the technology and medicine by our Art for War, the expensive learning of old for the Lu who lose. Expensive is the word cloud to learn, experience and worthy of attention, particularly good and heavy with word generation, the words of kings, and the Qi of hope.

For the Qi of Hope is the distinguished door and prestige, high prices, yet the birds cheap for the relatives of status to sell to the Lu as words of conduct, duties and unity of family words, names and fiscal policy by the twisted pairs the ancients cut with talent, money and materials by the rich trade from the east and the politics of serving our will to be exhaustive by changing trends by this chaos.

Money and goods, exhausted by words and times; anxious and bring people serious difficulties, and fast and fierce storms, and pioneers of benefit with the currency of effectiveness in the tables of the times and situations taught [by our banks and auction houses and Lu losses], learnt and guarded by the masonry that closed the ancient corpses in their coffins and tombs [ridges], concealing the quantifiers of the field of the science of change theory and chaos as a funeral service for the hostages of the sun. That enslaves the Lu in service as present labour of our Art for War by the force of the turning of the tides, the interaction between objectives, their acceleration and deformation, the effectiveness of all things in production and control. The forces of human and horsepower by the performance and orchestration of our amounts of gas in the administration of suffering by poison, election, awards and knowing meaning by education from our night schools, on the Oriental texts to study, the natures and grades between the ends, the ranges and the dark from the Oriental originals of wild understanding and tolerance. The type [and spirit of our ink] of the foundation of the Lu Lord, initiation, and draft membership to good reason and colour by illumination from inside, as if accepted by the ancients and a brother of the court to the ground, as an accepted incomer insider, in a baptism to the ancient plot of the virtual font of stone in interpretation of the Family.

As a master of the specialised knowledge, not wild and knowing the poultry, the night schools, the methods, the road and the ink, and that living can as a family of the private schools the duties of conduct, the names of the families and altering words for which there are fees of money to learn, time, the consumption of things, and without money the illumination disappears in crosses [of conduct] to go with. Such as one of the four Mandarin sounds, the verbs related to the walking step, the verbs of trends, the role of drama as an actor, to get rid of, losing your skin [to be initiated and reborn], knowing the times of winter and spring [difficult beginnings and nourishing; liberation through contentiousness to a purity of universal conscientiousness]; the different categories of time. The direction of the road, the travelling, the associated logic and critical reasoning and the seven celestial goods, as the reasoning of the highest level for the only ones, the public, the altering families, and the fees, broken and incomplete for the only ones by the vehicle that stops and strikes absolutely; the Horse.

For the Horse is the big, the bee; the spoon; for people to ride; and to pull things; and match the bristles of the hair [as an allegory of the word cloud].

The horse is a [developing] helmet [mind protection] for the arrows of a crossbow, or the halberd cross bar, promoted in initiation and induction, of the loaded hearse, hidden by a cover, to deceive by concealment words sculls [Oars, slots for livestock to feed] for a vessel is propelled by sculls. A scull is a spoon-bladed oar, [a horse bladed knife of wood] for the Lu. An ornament for the livestock to feed [by this winnowing oar] of the masonry, that conceals the wooden framework of the ancient signs. As quantifiers by attributes to the larger field, the illume of words and the smell of the cross, to go with the oriental sounds of logical reasoning and critical thinking of the six dimensions of the cube.

§12.4

The winds are used for directing instructions in our Art for War, and also wins by the old read of a long time. Then words blunt the stupid with stagnation, the Lu become slow and sluggish, and not sharp with clumsy mouths by our Art for War, frustrated by our hidden calligraphy with a stroke broken off, pressing unsmooth cadence, breaking to folding and failure and injury by the loss of sharpness, confidence and feeling sensitive by our attack, for which the treatment is in the study of our ancient books. The medicine to our poison, blows and powers of creations of difficulties by the walls of masonry around the cities of Lu that govern the Lu, by the forces of time and words, and thereby an ordered chaos that bends by our bow surrender, by a loss of heart. Poor words: this is the reason the Lu people have been disgraced. We driving our Horse at the Lu, creating chaos and injustice, and the Lu bending by our songs; stretched like drummed leather that we beat and extended to frustration and pride.

For a long time violence for the Lu has been with the exposure to sun, with a strong sunshine. Yet by such exposure the Lu do not have the pictures from the papers the dew reveals for blue veins that tramp, damage and spoil everything, in a temper, impatient in a jump to thunder, by the divisions of our teachers by our Art for War, that mentors brothers and sisters of our ancient laws, medicine, time and words by the music and poetry used by birds that soar the feet on the way by our arrows day and night.

Heroes are blunt instruments of our Art for War.

Frustrated by the sharp, bent to their disgrace, by the thundered turn of the tide and the force of our effectiveness and use of Satan. For "Satan" means the force that exhausts the heart, by fingers that point and reprimand, that can be extensively seen with eyes and heard as smells, as gambles, and wide games to use up the Qi of the Lu.

For Satan is a titan that uses up goods by time, words and various ancient songs with doors that multiply by winds of disadvantage, the ancient cover for defeat, that bullies people by this business of disease, fatigue and wisdom from the coded source of night wisdom and our competent conjunctions.

Although conjunctions by our corresponding sparrows of even if, make the Lu people dead, yet still alive, by birds that soar Lu heads, as do not words can good Qi, and by our rearing horse carry on!

Therefore, our Art for War by inducing unexpected things for the Lu making them dead in heart and mind, and by famous smells. To hear things is a timely pass in this poultry dance and clinic to smell the meaning of the words, by calligraphy strokes, that make fun of the poor, making them clumsy and stupid, slow in speed of mind, in print and writing clever together, and so we laugh at the altering skills of a long time and also.

Long-time heroes in our Art for War and wisdom of music and medicine is our Li by altering Heroes [the husband husbands] to a land of doubting sheep by song generation and only one, as our Art for War.

§12.5

For is the old handicraft of processing the square, and this is the industry of the big guns, the canons. In the art of finished products, are the immortal goods, the Heroes of Chaos, of our own powers of creation of chaos with whom we fight the Lu people by our Art for War:

Whereby we encircled the Lu by the sun, as if the Lu were the centre of the universe, and the sun revolved around them. And this is our gold, by our higher levels of understanding movement, time and progression that the Lu do not understand, and by our patience in the study of cosmic order and words of hidden meanings.

Where use of our Art for War alters the laws of the universe, the planets, and the sun and moon, for the Lu.

Qi is the driving horse, the spread of reputations, longing for hearts, and inquisitive minds, to leather by our instrument, as a vehicle of thousands of permutations.

The leather is the changes of the vehicle of thousands of permutations.

The band brings the juice, as the point to face and use as a guide and collar, containing energy that attaches words as thorns as a burden to pull out money, wearing the worn by our ancient dagger.

Silk and cotton cloth are line made things; they are the reason for the clothing; and thus, the collar, from the illumination of the ancient scapular bones to the cross that reaches by the vertex of the foot Absolutely [by our organisation].

For the Absolute means holding the absolute principles of political, philosophical and theological matters and control, and using such to endorse our political power as the true elites of nobility, for monarchy is its form [and shape] and winds direction and thereby we act as if gods in this business of knowing.

The simplified characters [are for the many] in our Art for War, who feed us profits in their taxation.

By time and words, by words inside, that are closed to the many, whereby our income is satisfied by dense seams and soles, and we enjoy the traditional drama of the role of the network the crossing and the road on the outer altered Lu. As fees for the costs of sacrifice by the Lu to our Art for War, as our guests and customers. That we bin in service of their obedience, for the Lu sacrifice is to an expensive Lord, where the best man phases the customers by altering the time in a marriage of east and west.

The Lu are glued as if by the unity of the rubber from the trees and the plywood, paint on the doors and windows, that liquid juice can, to be used after the medicine, with lacquered barks, enveloped in the carving and grinding, by the altering equipment of life, death and woods, and therefore the priming materials to teach and to use.

The car, is the turn of the body of the text, the rotating bed of the machine of the juice container of the spinning of juice. The drive of the emperor's carriage, and the crack of cruel death before the lessons of the heavenly stems of illumination and the altering limitations as our salary and bearing on the Lu. By cardinal winds on the hostages encircled by the sun, as united school fees for the masses, and our gold as is our insights to the chaos, and we knowing that the Lu are satisfied with promises of a life after death from the cross [of words and ideas] for the altering masses, by division, by teachers who lift words to heaven and carry on our Art for War.

Chapter Thirteen

§13.1

Therefore, "In the Beginning" was a start [to initiation to our organisation;] as well, at the opposite end [of the Silk Road]. Just as anger [*menis*] in crisis.

Using our ancestors to create the weak by our complex of times, and the limited just square as enlightenment for those who only realise the spring silkworms of death, by silken lines, that side to do by insight and tears and can the Lu by the pages that start, "In The Beginning". As a testament to our ancient powers of creation, and twisted pairs from our word cloud and call, that was floated sky words by our ancestors who were the inventors of this artful heaven. And the measure [the Homer], our ancient strategy, plan and work on the Hostages of the Sun as the policy and our plot of measure, time and chaos its seed.

Heroes are old people in servitude to us as a pull for improper courage by classical words of heaven and earth, with the wife of the spouse held as if hostage to the music and song. Not for the sheep, by our Art for War, wisdom and the temple of our ancestors who count [and secretly planned harm for others, by measures and soft reading embedded] and win by connections that compliment and, get it.

As if trees with extra branches of knowledge to meanings that seem otherwise unrelated as our Art for War and wisdom of our temple who count soaring birds a victory by getting it! [Satisfying meanings] that countless [for the unaware], as the will of the night school and also.

The masses [at the temples] count as our victory.

Less count as birds that soar us to victory by a wisdom of conditioned situations described in classical words and unspeakable for the Lu, promoting the zenith of unity in knots and riddles that count almost as language aids of classical rhetoric, towering depression, by our ancient call in question.

As the body of generation to this healthy altered view of odd things and understanding a negative victory [over only one] in seeing the revealing present of time by all elements of thinking and carrying on our Art for War.

§13.2

War for war by sly sorts of things is the Way of and also.

Therefore, unexpected things are our weapon in the chaos we create, that we can, by our wisdom of time as a show, to point things out, by birds that soar and can use wisdom and show the words of altering birds that soar with use near, by our ink, and wisdom, and show from far away esoteric words of altered wisdom as light words, for the near, as our profit and benefit is using wisdom as a lure in chaos, and wisdom to take by our methods reality and thereby the wisdom of the prepared. Pre-arranged and installed by our long-winded Art for War.

Strong wisdom of changes to escape and avoid the disease; an angry wisdom that scratches by altering cuts, the humble by an arrogant wisdom that changes, lost by a wisdom that altered labours; dear wisdom altered from the oriental wisdom of the woman who suffered from a lack of good education and not open teachers.

Study the ancient books, they document the attacks and the books of medicine, the winds, the knots and be prepared for preparation to the back opera of an independent repertoire of citation, allusions and the ground; and the track to marry to birds that soar by hidden meanings, the healthy words as medicine for our Art for War, and the altered families that win by birds that scream, and can time; and to pass is to know also.

§13.3

Measure, is by our accounting and homers of profits to listen with obedience to the words that ting the ancient bells.

Yes, for altering potential, by showing the situations of the times to the bitter music, altering knots of ancestral food and wine as secondary words of assistance to the winds that alter the outsiders by words [added from above, by our word cloud] with potential by reasoned benefit of wisdom, and a system that alters and regulates rights [of knowledge] by also.

§13.4

Therefore, we made changes to things and altered texts to confuse time, create chaos and make profits, by altering the hearts and minds of men by a school of specialised education as our Art for War, by altering to, and Homers of [partial] measurement in our accounting of time, as our ancient plot, wisdom, twisted cables, cabals of winds and the want of classifications for situations and shaping potentials.

By a secondary language of hidden words and syntax as a sin tax for the sacrifices of the sun, that on the surface make no real meaning, that with brightness the hidden, esoteric value is revealed to the blinded, and such is the gold of poetry and songs, the nature of the lord of the power of our creation, the logical reasoning of comparative meanings, and having the party method, and the situation to change the disease by song generation by the Way.

The will, the logical reasoning of the degrees of time and the comparison of meaning of having the two, and not the only one, and can. Hostages of the Sun are ground by the logic of words, get it?

Laws made by a logic of rows and columns as if soldiers ranked and filed by our Art for War for the masses by the strength of the ancient cooked books.

Debilitating by a death of logic in the practice of raw silk and the skill of the old alien reward, a pun and a penalty of logic the ancients cooked with insights and intelligence, of dark and bright, of sun and moon, by universal forms of reference, by generation to logical knowledge that is a victory over the negative interpretation that we allow to carry on.

The will and strategy of the night school is to listen selfishly to homer, that is part of the fool measure and accounts for degrees of time, plan and strategise, using alternating twos to decide, contemplate and assess the indispensable, the potential, and the resistance in the strategy to gain victory by altering delays to levels of leaving and the steps to the higher levels of understanding meaning that we keep hidden to pull and arrest the

Lu that the Lu receive and accept, and thus we are saved by what the Lu do not read.

The will of the birds that soar, by listening to and influencing politics, instilling an obedience that is made to be the accepted view of others with ears that accept the sound of the forces of the horse that we selfishly hear, measure and use, altering the stubborn with no intention to change by winds of twos. Therefore, the Lu lose by the crossing and altering strokes of our office, and go with trends in this drama as actors on the Way to our Mandarin sounds.

§13.5

The Way is the road and direction taken together.

The law, the rationale of the righteous, that helps to gain and helps to lose in academic ideology, where a pass is to have learned and been repaired by the method of the method, the doors, and technology we call our medicine from the superstitious disabilities of the consistent will of our organisation of doors, to what is said in the language of affection and apology, and thanks. In pencil lines for children and is the quantifier of two doors, a measurement unit for beneficial changes and also, is our ancient dagger, by making the fox and the porcupine of ancient times in words and printed sheets as orders for the superior to lower the method of life and change by the ancient evening method of seasons of time and the chaos of good smells and bad, and a system of governed by songs, and of other interpretations, for working masses and fishery, by what appears on the surface as non-military methods to the multitude, in verses to correct the wrongs, by tiger skins of life and death. As a gift for the Lu, convenient, yet comparative by conjunctions, by sponsoring praise and "rather" use. As if a case for fish by Mandarin aids of expressed questions in laments, rhetoric and tones and degrees of time. By our published tables, classes, organisation and dispensing medication as the ordered way and the vehicle of carrying on in this special way with the Lu mind and thinking in order, that we achieve our desired purpose and conscious efforts for the psychology of the Lu state we have in mind, out of words with no wine as a poetry, to guess from the outside the true meanings that we have in mind, as also our desires.

Altering by music of lost texts and one road and not two, and not flexible to knots in the weaving of good reason, and asleep to the death of the warrior, the Hero, as the sacrifice of life's determination. By our Art for War as an altering punishment for the Hostages of the Sun. As our strategy on the ground, by the leaves we altered and took away versus altering health, by a wisdom of birds that soar the masses [in temples] in fear and danger, and by surprising tellers of death by song for the Hostages Encircled by the Sun.

Overcast and in the concave to the knowledge of sun and moon that the ancients pretended and installed for the Lu as an attack of madness, a depression by words that tell lies and cause Lu's hearts and minds to die.

Cold by the clothes and poor scholars to the prostitution of critical thinking and reasoning time systems from canons as maps and leathers to the ancient orders that conduct the belt of limitation of constitution by type and ground leaves and also.

Time systems that table judgements to questions of passages as a recognition of situations in words, and also the ground by far and near and the spirit of ink.

As insurance to risk by change that is easy for us, made wide by the Temple [the round cottage of the old school, as a reference to the nunnery and the child, the gold] and the narrow – the street song prostitutes of evil death music for the sleepy and the stubborn, who have lost, in a sacrifice of life's determination, through Heroes as our Art for War, as Hostages encircled by the sun, as our strategy on the ground, and health, and also.

The will of the school above the school by wisdom of the forces of the machine that reasons time, the journey by foot and the faint words that stretch confessions by strokes and meanings and pieces and pigeon by extension of benevolence.

By a hard shell as if a walnut that is hard to eat and part, and disables the brave by our Art for War, by powerful strictness over the dense and the music of also.

As law by song, wine, system and spectrum high and widowed, to bend to the Lu straight by our crooked means as an art form of words and a leather by systematic canons, officially by the Way and Dagger, and use of the Lord, dead tablets, wood and also.

Where the music cuts the words of our Art for War by our twilight will of birds that soar and smell with the nose and ugly reputation of famous people who hear things and pass our clinic; the strong minded to our timely poultry dance of altering knowledge by a victory of birds that soar knowledge by birds of prey in victory over this carrion [and carry on].

§13.6

Therefore, with the ancient words were instead hired as a vehicle to the flock, in an industry of service to our creative Lu Lord, with due care and attention, and the Lu thinking of superstitions and reading of the bogeyman of wrath [*menis*]. Of whom the Lu ask pity, whereby we invented this sickness of hearts and minds deliberately with our steps, sealing and leather-bound papers that Lu might stick to their belt, of our reasoned edge and powers of creation of unexpected things that change as the Lu sacrifice their lives by the words of our Art for War altering through time and elemental changes to bitter conflicting music in the Lu social phenomena and activities, by the people who love situations and the Thing.

The altering school of specialised education, in the comparison field as a preparation for below from above by our Art for War of two measured daggers of a plot, wisdom and twisted cable of two windy situations, shaping and forming potential by music, the medicine and divisions.

One golden child [progeny] from the poetry cloud of the Way of direction.

The twilight language of secondary words for the Hostages encircled by the Sun, and not knowing of the universal orchestration of our movement and time.

That time has a currency and dimensions in songs in a hidden secondary language and sin tax of brightness to the ground, as a blanket on the board, with a purpose as our foundation to politics by the Lord of our creation of governing words, as a platform from before to place the progeny of the body of the texts, of our ancient classics and the illumination of the forms and flowers in the music of language of hidden meanings in songs as the will of our bees in the wind.

Elemental to our Art for War by primed words in a code of division by law.

§13.7

And so, the old concession to escape is the progeny of our ancient bamboo branches and their progeny of gold that teaches chaos by soft reading of the order of things late at night by the ancient mother of the earth who sets things to progeny and flourishing by the school of sound and vowels and defines the poultry by the system of the secondary language. That by moonlight we see and hear her hidden meanings in what we call the elemental music of the sun – the illuminated golden progeny from the word cloud creation of our ancient thinking relatives.

Our Art for War by grinding the ancient bones of contention as a sacrifice as altering music and medicine for big Heroes to pass in a horse opera and novel of what is best for all humanity to change the thing and love situations as an industry of nature.

That humanity might change and find another way out for the dead to the music, lost texts and knots. The sleepy who only know one road and the hard sell of a sacrifice of life's determination, creating dead warriors as Heroes, that punish the Hostages of the Sun in their memory to what was lost for the stubborn, by our Art for War in sacrifice of health and that many be also saved by knowing what is true and what is fake. And the progeny of the old horse, that nag, that makes a country slaves by altering the Way and the Dagger, in death by the wooden horse of the Ilium bone of ancient contention.

In presumption of timely opportunity, and knowing, and understanding the cardinal directions of winds, and thus the skilled manipulation of the future, between what the many know as our creation of Heaven, and the many, that we know are sheep. For whom lies by our coercion a deception we have deluded to this time.

By the birds that soar the masses and can prey as carrion in meticulous observation in a metaphor for smart people who should feel free to visit, in investigation of the rock festival, and bone radicals that pen autumn measures, as plots by effortless brush strokes on silks, as our amenable Art for War.

Epilogue
The Plot, The Disease and The Cure

§14

To kill off the great spirit and steal the enormity of the universal soul is the work of traitors who seal their mouths.

For they cherish all of what these matters contain. As if they have a belief in what they do is right, and that they, and only they, are correct in their behaviour.

This takes place like this by their rules and laws and regulations, and grades placed upon our common humanity.

As if such things as the great spirit and the universal soul are goods to trade in.

For only them only to open and pour out.

For such thieves and traitors to common humanity only correct by their perceptions of mistaken judgements.

Yet, reality is the other way around.

Such matters and actions require to be opposed and rebelled against, by careful reflection and consideration of their gravity.

And this can be confirmed by Fanqie – in the ancient way of specifying the meaning and reading of the characters.

For the medicine is a cure, a doctor that will heal such ills in our humanity.

Creating peace and tranquillity by a great re-birth.

That we might understand the shape of the tree and the brush used in the books, and read with dragon's fire, that we might possibly handle and govern and act like this – like what is truly written in such books.

For it should be the case to be in accordance with heart, mind intelligence, and soul.

For one can follow the traces of such impressions as if footprints.

For both the human body and the lay of the land.

For both comprise of circumstances, conditions and situations.

Both form and create; exhibit and show.

And so, we can compare to the matrix, knowing the universal laws and the punishments. The semblance of the great and the shadow of the shade - but without the angles.

And, by such methods diagnose by appearance!

Men achieve good results, and flourish when times are not negative, and such is the method to save, and by such rescue attend to the present – by heart, mind intelligence and soul, as one alone.

And such is the great work, the labour to toil. That it will bring exhaustion to the weak. Create thirst in the heat of the day, and hunger as if starving by a famine in a cold wintry chill of the night.

Yet, by such hazards, there is a tiny crack. A strategic point, that leads to a narrow pass, by which one can turn to hide, and thus escape and avoid such misfortunes.

Where one is never to feel sadness nor to be heart broken by such bitter cold – all because of knowing deeply the extremes of your heart, mind intelligence and cold.

All of which helps one obtain – a self – something that is inside of us – that we already know.

If supposing an anger filled with hate, bitter hardships and suffering one can observe in others – perceive this gift. The force to make do. To know the will of heaven, and know of fate, and know for certain.

For in such a person, their body is pregnant with moral character and ability, that protects against pity and regret, and guards against the culprits in this sad murder by these traitors of the universal soul.

For it is good fortune to be concerned. And this is the beginning of such supposing.

For the Eternal Feminine is Queen – she looks back and looks after. She looks in front when you are proceeding.

Well, look out for her and respect her rewards of kindness, that you will find satisfying and pleasing.

Show distain for what is happening at large, accumulate, plan and consider. That is to say think of the relationships of things, as if a thorny tree and listen to the pedigree of all that is relative. To reach what should be the case for everyone.

Yet wait alone, with the universal wisdom of knowledge and intelligence. Knowing the stupidity and foolishness of the barbarian tribes. Using flowery illustrious ancient Chinese as your friendly company in good fraternity to control and regulate this thorny tree of hatred, enmity and resentment.

For the ugly woman is beautiful and seductive. You the infant immature longing to excel in leadership and wealth yet poor impoverished and needy. Having discovered that the expensive and valuable is worthless and cheap.

And so, ask for her morality and kindness, and show distain for the rest. And by such method you will be saved and thereby rescued, if you seek and request, from the comings and goings of adversity, difficulties and distress. Illnesses, suffering, bad and evil people, hatred, anger, jealousy and over exertion.

And, thereby benefit in hardship and suffering, by finding the spiritual world and cherishing it as a saviour and rescuer, that relieves and helps, by universal widespread sincerity and honesty in a pledge of mapping thereto heart, mind intelligence and soul.

By a hidden secret, that feels compassion, kindness and benevolence, peace and tranquillity – by an elder broad ranging respect.

To open and expose previous demands as negative desires and negative purposes.

By settling with the universal spirit, against those who undertake most certainly to create this sickness and disease.

And thus, to rule and administer a cure.

To heal as if a doctor, bringing peace at the highest levels for all in the name of the universal state by your surgery. For now, and for all our tomorrows in the illumination of true beauty for our common humanity.